BATTLE SCARS A

CW00723196

B. Stephens.

BATTLE SCARS
AND
PONDWEED

Charles Draper

PHARAOH PRESS
AND
LIVERPOOL BOOKS ONLINE

Battle Scars and Pondweed

First Published in 2002 Pharaoh Press
and liverpool books online
Copyright © Charles Draper 2002

The right of Charles Draper to be identified as the author of this
work has been asserted in accordance with sections 77 and 78 of
the Copyright Designs and Patents Act 1988.

ISBN 1-901442-25-X

Printed and bound by Antony Rowe Ltd, Eastbourne

Acknowledgements

Throughout the time it has taken me to put this book together, I have been fortunate in having the assistance of a number of people without whom I would have been left floundering in the dark.

I am delighted, therefore, to have this opportunity to thank the following people: the staff of Crosby Library for their courtesy, patience and co-operation as I sought to confirm in their archives what my memory could not recall unaided; Bob Wright who let me have the run of his excellent social history museum in Little Crosby; and John O Toole, whose editorial guidance, constructive criticism and encouragement proved invaluable.

I am also indebted to my children, Miles, Mark and Jodie who bullied me unmercifully when my enthusiasm wanted but were courteous enough to laugh in all the right places.

Finally, to my wife Carol, who played so much a part in my growing up and has been beside me for all the many years since.

BATTLE SCARS AND PONDWEED

Chapter 1

From my perch, high up in the hay loft in Cambridge Road corporation yard, I looked across the railway line toward Brook Vale and over to the ever advancing 'Whabb's' tip. Even from where I sat I could see wisps of smoke and flame breaking through the surface of the compressed rubbish. Soon the Fire Brigade would arrive and spend the afternoon hosing it down. It was a regular occurrence and sometimes it smouldered for days.

In the distance I could see bin wagons entering the tip at Beech Road in Litherland. Crawling, roller-coaster fashion, over the uneven ground toward the canal side of the valley, they disgorged their contents where directed, and where later I would be rummaging. Slowly, the empty wagons lurched back toward the gate, leaving clouds of swirling, choking dust in their wake. Further up the valley cows roamed freely, heads lowered, chomping on grass that soon would be denied them.

Mick barked up at me to let me know it was time we were off exploring and together we ran across the bridge which spanned the Southport to Liverpool railway line. Cutting through the playing fields of Waterloo Grammar School we headed for the ditch by the allotments to hunt for frogs, and also to check on the partridge nest I'd found last week.

I had arrived on the scene, three weeks earlier than I should have, at Elm Drive Seaforth, in April 1937, and was pencilled in as number six of seven. I was pink and healthy when born, but within six weeks I caused my parents considerable anxiety by coming down with whooping cough.

Alder Hey hospital was my home for the next week, but when my mam was informed by the staff that the only remedy was to patiently remove the offending phlegm from my throat, she decided that could be done at our house under her watchful

1

eye. Wrapping me in a protective blanket, she picked me up and took me home.

In the days before preventive medicine was discovered, whooping cough could be a killer. As there was no real cure as such, it had to run it's course. All my mam could do was look after me and hope for the best. Our local GP, Dr Mann from Crosby Road, advised my mam to take me to the beach when the tide was coming in and hold me facing the river; it was something to do with the 'ozone' he said. I'm not sure that breathing in large gulps of Irish Sea air helped, but I did improve and eventually made a complete recovery.

A few months later I contracted diphtheria which brought me close to death's door. Fortunately, I wasn't close enough to gain admittance and again I recovered. There were other childhood illnesses to contend with but after the two main events, the rest were 'also rans'. The fact that I'm here at all bears testimony to an iron constitution and an unshakable faith, in which, if I was sadly lacking, my mam had in abundance!

At five, my 'academic' career started at the Star of the Sea Primary school, Seaforth, but by five-and-a-half I was ready to call it a day. Bigger boys (and some girls!) kept knocking me to the floor. I decided that enough was enough and declared my intention to fight back. I cast down the gauntlet and there was a scramble to pick it up! Consequently, I had to take on all comers. Any free time I had seemed to be spent fighting and wrestling in the dirt, but thanks to a reasonable rate of success, the message was driven home and I was left alone.

I didn't like school, partly because I wasn't too bright at most subjects, but more so because I found it all a bit dull. There were, though, a number of occasions when I enjoyed going to school in anticipation of certain lessons. Walking to the Mission Hall on Linacre Road to attend woodwork was a subject I enjoyed immensely, and was always sorry when the instructor brought the lesson to an end. I would have been content to stay there all day!

Another 'lesson' I always looked forward to, was going by train to Southport baths. For me, a train journey was a treat at the best of times, but to visit the baths as well was an extra thrill! Once Mr Breen, our teacher, threw a two shilling piece into the water and dived in after it.

"Whoever finds it can keep it," he shouted, but while we searched the bottom of the pool in vain, he had already secreted the coin in the folds of an old war wound in his side! However, it was after school hours that I lost myself in a childhood wonderland.

The war years played an enormous part in my childhood, but it was the aftermath that provided me with an adventure playground that most children today could only dream about. Bombed houses galore! There were empty cellars and staircases that wound up and up and creaked ominously as we ran around exploring deserted rooms. A rope proved a valuable asset in situations like these, because once it was attached to a beam you could swing out of one window and, given the correct momentum, sail through the window into the next room, completely unaware of the danger! Any window pane that had somehow escaped the bomb blast were targets at which to throw stones. Partly damaged walls, or even whole houses, simply begged to be demolished.

The authorities were in total confusion just after the war and with so much property to pull down or renovate, they were no doubt quietly pleased that gangs of marauding children were levelling parts of the borough! It saved them the expense of pulling them down and provided a situation of which we took full advantage.

We invented many daft games, like who would be the first to knock every bit of glass from a chosen frame with our 'catties'. Even the smallest piece left in would disqualify you. Another challenge was to split into pairs and see who could demolish a downstairs wall the quickest. Whether any of the walls were load bearing or not never entered our heads, because we didn't

3

know of such things. We just hammered away with iron bars or lumps of wood until it was reduced to a heap of rubble!

The rickety houses that draw tourists in droves to theme parks, we had for real and they were the ultimate hide and seek venue. We often played in a large derelict house on Sandy Road. It was a three story house and a favourite pastime was to pop our heads out of one of the many holes in the roof and flick small stones at people waiting at the bus stop below. My friends and I played for hours, oblivious to time or danger.

One day, the whole of the top floor collapsed into the cellar not long after we had left. I shudder to think of the outcome if it had happened twenty minutes earlier! Strangely, none of the bombed and flattened houses were cordoned off or fenced in. Children were not as cosseted in those days and I must admit I have had an affinity with derelict houses ever since. Collecting bonfire wood posed no problems in the early post war years. There were plenty of gutted houses to strip. The amount of quality timber we ripped out and burnt doesn't bear thinking about!

Once, we found a quantity of bullets in the cellar of a bombed house in Cambridge Road. We played for hours throwing them against the wall, the occasional bang being our reward. After one particular bang, Bill Seddon clutched his thigh and fell to the floor.

"Argh!" he shouted.

When we looked there was an angry red mark on his leg, just above his knee. His face was twisted in agony.

"Cor, it doesn't 'alf sting!" he said, through tightening lips. It was obvious that it needed more than a good rubbing with a dock leaf!

"You're best goin' home and getting a cold flannel on tha'" I said, the voice of experience. "Me mam does that for me whenever I bang me 'ead and it always seems to work" Tommy Hughes, full of cold, was watching over my shoulder and his nose was dripping onto Bill's injured thigh. Sniffing deeply, he shrugged, unimpressed.

"I had a cut last year that was dead better than tha'!"   Bill didn't come out for the remainder of the day but the next morning he showed off a wonderful red and blue, swollen bruise, which we all jealously admired. Of course, he was particularly proud of his 'gunshot wound' and refused to wear long trousers for weeks, even on the coldest days. Such blissful ignorance! We were completely unaware of where the spent bullets ended up. I probably strafed the area with more live 'ammo' in those few days than Hitler's Luftwaffe did throughout the entire war!

Living in Sandringham Road after the war was a happy time of adventure and discovery. We would collect frog spawn, watching in fascination as each day a new development unfolded, or sometimes we'd go 'bird nesting'. As it was still fresh in our minds, we would often go to the sand hills at Seaforth or Waterloo and take on the might of the German Army, re-enacting the invasion of Normandy. Our days were full but they were never long enough.   There are few experiences to equal a group of young pals out seeking adventure. Simple things like tree climbing, conker gathering and sticky bud raids were great fun. We used to explore dense woods and play hide and seek in thick ferns. Once a nest of red ants caused me to jump up and reveal my hiding place, and I paid the penalty by being pelted with pine cones! We ran through sandhills chasing lizards, only to find with horror that when you captured your prey he applied his ultimate escape plan and left his tail in your hand! Years later, this all came flooding back to me when I embarked on a mission of mercy, killing hundreds of rabbits affected with myxamatosis.

Using a small net attached to a long cane, we would fish for hours in Rimrose Brook behind Sandy Road, and follow its winding course through the tunnels beneath the railway line, catching sticklebacks and 'Jack Sharps'. The wriggling fish would be dropped into a jam-jar, into which we would add a water beetle for company and a piece of weed for decoration.

Arriving home we'd be covered from head to toe in battle scars and pond weed, which, once it dried, was harder to remove than paint!

My scruffy appearance often warranted a clout from my mam and I never managed to dodge her. She had this uncanny ability to clip you around the ear without even looking at you, irrespective of which direction you came from! Later though, when I was cleaned up and all was forgiven, I sat at the table listening to 'The Man In Black' on the wireless. The coals would glow orange-red in the grate and as my eye-lids became heavier, I reflected on the days adventures and considered new ones to come. I also wondered how the hell I was going to tell my mam the jumper she'd finished mending only the day before, was now at the bottom of the canal!

Chapter 2

We stopped swinging around the lamp-post to allow Mr Porter to pass. I stared quite fascinated at the neatly pinned, half empty, trouser leg. Propelled forward by his crutches, his incomplete body swung rhythmically as he turned into the gateway where he lived.

It was only after I had asked my dad about how Mr Porter had lost his leg that I became aware of other men who had limbs missing or behaved strangely. I was then better able to understood why the man I often saw on Crosby Road shook his fist toward the sky, before retreating into the nearest shop doorway until whatever horror he imagined, had passed. People stared and quickened their step and we would snigger and run away feigning terror! We used to circle a forefinger near our temples when we saw Mr Aston arguing with lamp-posts. We were only young boys who knew no better, but today I can reflect on our behaviour and feel a little shame.

Although maimed survivors from the two world wars were a common sight when I was young, they are less frequently seen today. Hopefully, the threat of global warfare will diminish and such sightings will, in future, be a thing of the past. We often saw men who spent the whole day sitting on benches in Bowersdale Park or Potter's Barn. Lost in thought, they would shake their head now and then and blink rapidly. Were they thinking back to a time when they had lived in an alien world of carnage and horror? Maybe they remembered the young men, some not much more than boys, who never returned to their homes and loved ones. Did they ponder on the unbelievable waste of it all?

It was only when the sun was setting that they made a move to go home. There were large numbers of men walking with the aid of crutches or skilfully manouvering wheelchairs in and out of shops. What did I know of such things then? I can look back now with new found knowledge, but back then, names like Passchendeale, Somme and Ypres meant nothing to me. I didn't know where they were! I gave up trying to think of answers. For a young lad not yet a teenager, there weren't any!

Our street party, held to celebrate the end of the war, was no different to any before or since. There was lots of jelly, lemonade and fairy cakes made by various neighbours. I remember we were lucky because the weather had stayed fine. It was a glorious sunny day and the bunting that had been strung across the road hung limp and still. People danced to scratchy records being played on an old wind-up gramophone, which was later replaced in favour of Mr Wilson's accordion.

Afterwards, we held games and races in the street. I won a fifty yard flat race and my prize was a pack of cards which, when you flicked them quickly, looked like a moving picture! During another tough race I was overstretching to reach the tape, when I fell and skidded along the gravel, grazing my knee to the bone and ending in a heap outside Mr Porter's house! It was the kind of graze that evoked sympathetic clucking from grown-ups and, once the pain had subsided, would be sported like a badge of honour among my mates! Everyone rushed to my aid and I felt like a hero. Mr Porter, who had been watching the fun from his gateway, turned to my mam, who had been fussing around.

"It's alright, Mrs Draper," he said quietly, "I'll take care of him. You go and see to the others". He turned to me saying, "follow me, young fella, me lad."

I followed him into the house, marvelling at how he moved so easily and quickly. He was up the steps and along the hall while I was still thinking about it! I was probably exaggerating the extent of my injury, as young boys tend to do, but even so, I could hardly keep up with him!

"You sit yourself there, Charlie boy," he said pointing to a large couch, "I won't be a minute."

I sat there sucking my breath in whenever it stung, trying not to cry, when Mr Porter came back carrying a bowl of warm water. Taking a square of white cloth he soaked it in what he called 'his special mixture' and placed it gently over my knee. He repeated this again and again and although I flinched more than once, it felt much better and I began to relax. Mr Porter looked up at me.

"You can cry if you want to, Charlie. It's nothing to be ashamed of, you know. Even grown men cry! I could tell you some tales." He remained silent for a moment and then he looked at me again, and thumping the stump of his leg, laughed. "I bawled like a baby when I got this, and I'll tell you something else," he leaned closer and whispered, "it wouldn't have done any good rubbing it with a dock leaf!" He laughed again and I laughed with him. "Tell you what. How about you and me have a nice cup of cocoa. What d'you say to that?" I nodded vigorously.

I stayed in Mr Porter's kitchen for the remainder of the afternoon, and he showed me photographs of when he was a young man working on a farm. I could hear the sounds of laughter from the street party coming through the open door, but I didn't care. I was content to stay where I was. We made toast from the fire and now and then he would tell me stories about the First World War, or as he called it, The Great War. He packed a pipe with tobacco, lit it and sucked on it until it glowed red. Soon there was a blue smoky haze in the kitchen and a rich syrupy aroma reached my nostrils. He told me of acts of heroism and how he lost his leg.

"I lost a lot of mates in those first few weeks, Charlie. Good mates. Men I'd joined up with and trained with. There's a bond between men thrown together like that, and when that bond is severed by a bullet . . ." he paused and looked at me, adding softly, "you feel empty, Charlie boy. Lost."

"How? . . ." I hesitated, not wanting to ask such a personal question, but he was a step ahead of me.

"What? Lose this bugger? Well, now, I'll tell you, Charlie." He settled back in his chair puffing contentedly on his pipe.

"We'd been ordered to advance toward a place called Zonnebeke. We moved forward at a slow pace and met with no opposition for the first couple of hundred yards. The birds were singing and I remember thinking what a lovely day it was. Not like a war at all. Then, it started. The air seemed full of angry bees and a couple of my mates got hit. It was hard to keep moving knowing your mates were wounded, but I couldn't tend to them 'cos we were told not to stop for anything. We made good progress toward a small wood and then I felt a thump on my leg . . ." He paused for a few moments. "I don't remember much after that. I woke up in a field hospital."

"Does it hurt now?" I asked.

"Only when I laugh, Charlie boy. Only when I laugh!"

I began to laugh and so did he until we were both laughing uncontrollably! Every now and then Mr Porter grabbed his stump, pretending it was hurting and that made matters worse. In the end I fell off the couch!

We became firm friends after that and I used to run to the shops for him, to get his 'baccy'. Afterwards, we would sit in his kitchen drinking tea and he would tell me stories about his army days and when he used to work on the farm. In the autumn of that year he asked me would I help him do some planting in his garden. He had acquired a lot of daffodil bulbs and, once he had chosen the site for planting, he went ahead of me making holes with his crutches in the soft peaty soil. I followed him with the bag dropping in the bulbs! Neither of us knew much about gardening and were disappointed with the result in the spring. Next door's daffodils were vigorous and tall and healthy looking, but Mr Porter's didn't fare too well at all. They were stunted and what flowers did emerge died quickly as though wanting to get the season over with. It was only when he decided to move them to a sunnier location we discovered I had planted them upside down! Mr Porter laughed so much he had to lean against the back door to stop himself from falling over!

He lived well into his eighties and I was a constant visitor, even into my teens. It came as a shock when his cousin told me of his death. He handed me a piece of shrapnel.

"Before he died, George said he wanted you to have this. He told me to tell you, this is the `bugger' that done him!"

I gazed at the evil looking piece of metal in my hand and smiled. Well, the 'bugger' may have taken his leg, but it left behind his warmth and his sense of humour. He was a fine man who had a fascinating personality and one I was happy to call a friend. I still have that `bugger' today!

Mrs Moss lived in Kinross Road, opposite where I lived. She was very old, although, how old I never knew. Even my mam could only say she said she was 'a good age'. When I was sent to the shops, my mam often asked me to call in to see if Mrs Moss needed anything, and I would go and tap lightly on the front door. When she saw it was me she would open it wide and smile encouragingly.

"Me mam sent me to see if you needed anything from the shops, Mrs Moss"

More often than not she would say that she had already been for her 'bits', but now and then if she needed some little thing she had forgotten, she would call me in and I would go through into the kitchen to wait, while she rummaged about in her purse for the money. I remember looking around the room at the many photographs that hung on the wall and along the top of the mantlepiece. It was always cosy and warm, and two clocks ticked in unison, intruding on the quiet of the kitchen. In one corner, a what-not, which looked cluttered with little china pieces and mementoes, sagged to one side. Only the chimney breast saved it from total collapse! Suspended from the ceiling, her clothes rack swung freely in the breeze that came through the open door. She always said the same thing when I was going. It never varied.

"Thank you Charles, and you must tell your mother 'thank you', too. Here," and she would press a ha'penny into my palm, "that's for you. Mind you spend it sensibly." Of course, I always thought that buying sweets was very sensible!

As a boy I must have looked desperately undernourished because people were always asking me in for hot drinks or giving me sandwiches and encouraging me to drink Bovril! Once, after returning with Mrs Moss' messages on a cold and wet Saturday, she asked me if I'd like some soup.

"I've just this minute made it," she said, "it's home made. Come in and have some. I'm sure it won't spoil your tea." I was always hungry anyway and it did smell wonderful. I exercised remarkable restraint by not bounding up the lobby ahead of her! She led me through to the now familiar kitchen and sat me at the table by the window, while she went into the back kitchen. The yard, like the rest of the house, was spotless and in the far corner stood two old dolly tubs filled with soil. In summer, as I recalled, they were filled with Marigolds and other plants and were a riot of colour. She came back carrying a tray and placed it in front of me. On it was a bowl of steaming soup and some bread cobs.

"There, you tuck into that. It'll do you good." When she saw me looking at the single bowl on the tray, she added hastily, "Oh, don't mind me, I've had some already."

As I ate the soup I looked around the room and my eyes rested on a photograph in the centre of the mantlepiece. It was of a man in army uniform standing behind a lady seated on a high backed chair. He was a tall man with a light complexion and the lady was very pretty with dark hair and a dress buttoned high to the neck. She followed my gaze.

"That was taken a long time ago, Charles. That was my Tom and it was taken on the day we became engaged." For a moment she had a far away look in her eyes. "He was taken from me in the war." Then she brightened. "Would you like some more? There's plenty and I won't eat it all."

I shook my head and explained I was full and after thanking her, went to see if the lads were ready to play out. I'd found an old football on the tip and although it was a bit soft, I was sure it would last for a few good kick-abouts! Jimmy had said it was no good, but when I pop a few shots into his goal, I thought, he'll soon change his mind!

> The clock on the mantle ticked loudly,
> But the old lady was lost in thought.
> To a time when young love, so long ago,
> Was the memory she sought.
>
> She smiled to herself as dancing flames,
> Cast shadows around the room.
> A time recalled to cherish,
> When their love began to bloom,
>
> And when he was called to fight,
> On a ship he had to sail.
> It took him to a foreign land,
> To a place called Passchendaele.
>
> News of his death in that dreadful place
> Was posted on a solemn board.
> She stood bewildered in rain soaked clothes,
> Surrounded by a weeping hoard.
>
> The wailing sound that rose and fell,
> Pierced her body like a knife,
> Until at last she turned away,
> Into a lonely life.
>
> The old lady sighing heavily,
> Drifted into deepest sleep,
> To dream of childhood and of happy times,
> And memories to keep.

The clock on the mantle chimed loudly,
A musical encore,
But it mattered not to the lady in the chair,
She couldn't hear it anymore.

Mrs Moss was found dead just a few hours after I had waved goodbye to her. Neighbours, chatting in groups with arms folded, nodded towards her house and pulled sympathetic faces saying she had died peacefully. One woman said there was still soup on the stove and remarked how lucky it was that the window cleaner had found her.

"Or the house could have gone up in flames!" Mrs Davis said, shaking her head sadly.

After a while people drifted away. Neighbours, realising there was no more they could do, sought comfort behind closed doors and I was left alone in the street. I looked over to Mrs Moss' house and noted the drawn curtains, and thought it was time I left.

I kicked my ball, rebounding it off garden walls until I reached home. Sitting in the garden with my dog I felt a sadness I had not experienced before. I put my arm around him and he looked up at me, his ears flat. `I hope my mates don't come to call.' I thought `I don't feel like playing out today.'

Chapter 3

Because Seaforth Barracks was a transit base for troop movements during and after the war, I came in contact with troops of different nationalities. Of course, streets ahead in popularity were the Americans, simply because they had more of everything than anyone else and could flaunt their generosity. Whenever we saw them strolling along the road we used to run over to them.

"Got any gum, chum?" we'd shout. They put up with us for ages and would always hand us a stick of gum or, occasionally, a whole packet. I was never that fond of 'chewy'. Once the sugary taste had gone, it tasted like rubber, so I used to ask them for a penny, instead!

"There you go, son," they'd say, but gradually their patience wore thin and we must have lost our cute, little urchin appeal, for after a while they started chasing us away. They were probably fed up with the war and being so far away from home for so long, and they began telling us to 'get lost' and 'you should be in bed'.

Italian prisoners of war on the other hand were a different kettle of fish. On my way home from school I sometimes joined groups of people outside the barracks gate in Claremont Road, where occasionally prisoners, perched on top of the gates, threw little packets of biscuits or single cigarettes into the crowd. It seemed inconceivable that prisoners could throw biscuits to me, when half the time they weren't available in the shops, even if you had the coupons! Mostly though, it was kisses they threw to young women who stood coyly giggling on the other side of the road.

Although the war was over bar the shouting, they were still officially prisoners of war. However, security was fairly lax and the authorities didn't seem too bothered if Italian prisoners enjoyed a certain amount of freedom. True, I had seen them gainfully employed brushing the streets, but more often than not they would wander up and down Rawson Road in groups, talking animatedly and even calling into the 'Doric' or the 'Claremont' for a swift half! They seemed an amiable and friendly lot, which is why my lower jaw dropped when Frank Lister sought me out one warm July evening and informed me that one had escaped!

"Escaped?" I echoed, "are you sure?"

"It's true. Arthur Jones told me. His brother lives opposite the barracks and he said the sirens were going last night, and that only happens when a prisoner has escaped".

"How does he know?" I snorted cynically, "no-one's ever escaped before".

"I dunno'. But that's what I 'eard" shrugged Frank.

On the way home I gave the situation much thought. The police and military would be out in force to ensure the recapture of the escapee and would be combing the docks and country-side. But they couldn't look everywhere and that's where Jimmy and I would come in. I was determined that if anyone was going to find that prisoner, it was going to be us. We were 'top-notch' trackers. Chingachgook in 'Last Of The Mohichans', had taught us all he knew! I could just see the headlines in the Crosby Herald:

"LOCAL BOYS CAPTURE VICIOUS ENEMY PRISONER".   -

Below the headline, there would be a picture showing a bemused POW being led away as we received our citations, and cheques, from the Mayor!

It was very dark, but we could see well enough to enable us to creep along the gullies in the sandhills at Seaforth. Every now and then the moon peeked from behind a cloud highlighting the wet surface of the beach, and light glistened from shallow pools left behind by the ebbing tide. Just visible on the sloping surface, I could make out the rows of concrete tank traps protruding from the sand like mini pyramids, which fortunately, were never tested in earnest. To our left the dark outlines of dock sheds were silhouetted for a moment, and from the warehouse roofs tall crane jibs bobbed up and down as though bowing to an unseen audience. The moon, deciding it had seen enough, darted back behind a cloud to rest.

"I'm not sure this is a good idea, y'know Charlie" Jimmy said anxiously.

"Why not," I whispered. "It makes sense. The police and the army are searching the docks and countryside but, it's possible that the 'Itie' is holed up in these hills waiting for his chance to make a break for it."

"Yeah, But where to? Where's he going to go? Even I know that he can't swim home from here! And don't forget that the area around the battery is mined". Again Jimmy sounded anxious. "Not knowing the area, he could get blown up!"

"Well, he's hardly likely to go climbing into places surrounded by barbed wire when he's just climbed out of one, is he? No, he'll lie low and wait for the right moment to leg it. Maybe steal a boat! Come on, we'll try over by Marine Gardens".

Alec Dobson and his fiancee, Sally Turner, had just left the Queen's picture house where they had watched Noel Cowerd clinging to a flimsy looking life-boat in a scene from, `In Which We Serve `. Alec was due to be 'demobbed' very soon and earlier in the evening Sally had agreed to marry him.

"That's marvellous" said Alec, hugging her tightly, "this calls for a celebration. What would you like to do?"

"Well, I don't want to go dancing or anything like that. I thought we could go to the pictures and maybe a fish supper after. Something nice and quiet"

"If that's what you want, my love, then that's what we'll do!" and he kissed her lightly on the lips.

Much later, when they were walking on the beach, the moon and the sea air, plus the fact that Alec was returning to his unit the next day, simply demanded that they enjoy a kiss and a cuddle in one of the sheltered sand gullies. They were swearing their undying love to each other, entwined in each others arms, when suddenly large amounts of sand rained down on them from above, followed by two boys who were running around in panic, and it was two boys Alec recognised!

"Hey!" he shouted, "what the hell..?"

The boys screamed in terror and were trying to scramble up the side of the gully. Alec made a grab for the nearest one, and Sally squealed as sand caked in her hair and poured down her neck.

"What's happening, Alec?" she shouted, her voice wavering anxiously, "who are those boys?"

"I'll tell you who they are!" he said through clenched teeth, as the two figures vanished in the gloom. "They are two scallywags who are in for a rude awakening when I get hold of them, I'll see to that!"

Half an hour and a near heart attack later, Jimmy and I were slumped over the drinking trough in Potters Barn gulping water from the tap!

We were sneaking about in the hills and had slid through the sharp `spider grass' into a gully using the soft sand to carry us down, when all hell broke loose. A tall figure suddenly sprang up in front of us. He yelled and made a grab for us. We yelled and made a run for it. I thought it was the 'Itie' and he was going to kill us, because we heard he had a knife, so I scrambled up the side of the gully. Only I didn't, if you know what I mean! The soft sugary sand just ran away beneath my feet and I was getting no-where. I felt my ankle being pulled at and it was then I found out your hair really can stand on end! Something flashed before me and at first I thought it was my life, but then I realised it was Jimmy! Here I was, on my own, in a deep sand gully, with an escaped enemy prisoner, who was growling and snarling and armed with a knife! It was all the impetus I needed and I flew around the sand like 'a wall of death' cyclist and leapt out of the gully like a kangaroo!

I ran in blind panic stumbling over unseen obstacles. Jesse Owen would have been pushing it to keep up with me! My chest felt as if it would explode, pushing the air out as quickly as I sucked it in! A branch from a tree in the park tugged at my jersey and I thought it was him. Afterwards, Jimmy said he had heard a scream and thought I'd been caught! I considered it prudent not to mention the branch incident. A minute later I joined Jimmy at the drinking trough but it was ages before either of us could speak.

"That must have been him!" I gasped. "That must have been the 'Itie! Did you see the size of the knife he had, Jim? He nearly had me, too! I've never been so scared in my life!"

"Me, neither, I couldn't move me legs, I thought he had hold of me!"

"C'mon, lets go to the police station and tell them we've found him!"

"Yeah, before he makes a break for . . ."

Jimmy paled and his lower jaw dropped open. His eyes had widened considerably, and with a shaking finger, was pointing at something behind me.

As I turned to see what was turning Jimmy's legs to jelly, we were grabbed by our coat collars and before we knew it our heads collided and I saw stars and cascading waterfalls in glorious technicolour!

"How d'you like that, eh?" a voice said. "Next time you decide to play commando, you make sure the fox-hole is empty!" And giving us a clout across the back of the head for good measure, walked through Potter's Barn arch and sauntered toward Woodland Road! We could hear the pair of them laughing and Alec remarked,

"That'll teach the little sods. Did you see their faces when we loomed out of the darkness?"

Sally, standing crossed-legged to avoid an accident, giggled uncontrollably, and at that moment our humiliation was complete. Or so I thought! The word got around and for weeks after, our mates took the mickey out of us unmercifully. What put the top hat on it was when Ronnie knocked at the door wanting to know if 'Mario' could come out after 'he's had his spaghetti'! There never was a mobilisation of the military and police, because no-one had escaped! The alarm bells that Arthur's brother had heard were fire alarm bells after a flair up of fat in the cook house, which quickly spread into the corridor! The Crosby Herald never ran a banner headline and I suppose we could count ourselves lucky really, because it could quite easily have read:

"PEEPING TOMS DETAINED ON BEACH!"

Chapter 4

"Get him out! He smells!" The cry echoed around the house, a sure sign that Mick had sneaked in. Mick was my mongrel dog and we were inseparable. Even playing with my friends, he would never be far from my side. He often gave me away when we played 'Hide and Seek'. If I found a thick bush to hide behind, he would sit close by, tongue lolling, an unmistakeable spoor to the 'seeker'. Threatening or throwing stones proved ineffective. There he was and there he was staying. When I was found and emerged furious from my hiding place, he would jump up and down, his front claws scoring red weals on my legs below my short trousers. Locking him up proved useless, for even if he was released hours later, he would make straight for Brook Vale and find me. I have been in the most unlikely places only to see him gallop toward me, his ears back, panting with an apparent look of complete joy on his face.

If I scolded him, he lay on his back, feet in the air, with his tail as stiff as a stick. After I relented, as he knew I would, I'd call to him slapping my thigh. "Come on, Mick!" I'd shout, and he would explode into life, his body twisting as he leapt licking my face and once again raking my legs.

Brook Vale was my 'Treasure Island', my 'Ali-Baba's Cave', my 'Sherwood Forest' or anywhere I wished it to be. It was there that I joined in mortal combat with 'Captain Kidd', slew dragons with St. George and sometimes defeated the evil 'Black Knight'. I was 'Zorro' and the 'Red Shadow' from 'Desert Song'. I pierced more of the Sherrif's men with my trusty long bow than Robin Hood ever did, though I never had the added perk of Maid Marion's hand to win! Mick was a poor substitute for a white charger but as he ran at my side I used to imagine he was 'Trigger' with me on his back.

The amount of Indians I massacred was awesome! There

wasn't a Redskin left to murder and pillage innocent settlers.The delighted townspeople insisted on making me Sherrif and on my next visit to Brook Vale, Jesse James' gang had little chance under my blazing guns and I was only slightly wounded when I rid the West, once and for all, of those dirty Daltons!

Mick would look at me with a puzzled look on his face as I staggered about feigning death from my wounds. It was only when the doctor's beautiful daughter came to look after me and I recovered, did he jump back with hind quarters in the air, front paws stretched out, in anticipation of another game.

Sandwiched neatly between the Leeds-Liverpool canal on one side and Waterloo and Great Crosby on the other, is a curved strip of land that followed the course of the Rimrose Brook, which we always referred to simply as, Brook Vale. My access to it was over the railway bridge from Sandy Road. It has altered now, of course, and has been largely landscaped. When Mick and I were running free it was a series of undulating grassy hills, valleys and streams hissing through masses of reeds, thick enough in places to offer nesting places for duck, moorhen and coot. At one end of the vale it was still farmland, while at the other end, a distance of about a mile, it had begun to give way to the ever increasing demand for space where the populace could dump their rubbish.

The place I spent most of my time was an area of some three or four hundred yards square, consisting largely of trees and scrub. In the centre was a large moss covered pond, flanked by willows and rhododendrons. It was there I learned the art of swinging across the pond on a rope. I also learned that if you didn't hold the rope high enough, you trawled the lake bottom with your backside! We had christened it 'King Kong's Island' and it was a wonderful place.

There I could lose myself in my own world of fantasy and only when I was going home, tired and dirty, did I become concerned about my appearance. I used to think that a quick splash on the face and knees would do the trick, but, of course, it never did. I could, it seemed, easily kid the townspeople from some obscure settlement, but never my mam. Mick used to reek of pond weed and mud, hence my mam's reaction to his presence. It never occurred to me to wash him, apart from the odd dip in the canal, which he hated.

As a footballer Mick was found wanting. He couldn't quite master the difference between defence and attack and had an annoying habit of picking up the ball and giving away penalties. Once, as we walked through Potter's Barn on our way to the sand-hills, he dashed onto the green and picked up the 'Jack' of an astonished bowler who had just delivered the perfect length. He rolled it gently at my feet, tail going like a piston, not realising he was being pursued by a florid faced man who gave me a clout around the ear for not having him on a lead. Mick peered from around the back of my legs where he had taken refuge, wondering what all the fuss was about.

However, as a cake thief, he reigned supreme! He would watch me going into Irwins at the corner of Grecian Street and Rawson road, then slip through the door after me. In a flash he'd be on the counter, grab a sandwich cake, and be out of the door before anyone realised what had happened. I would stand whistling up to the ceiling, denying him `thrice'! But I was soon on his trail to see if he had left me any!

In later years, when I'm ashamed to say I outgrew him, I saw less and less of him. I began a career as a seaman, and when I returned home from some trip or other, his tail and enthusiasm were still evident, but he was now very old. After one particular voyage I returned home to be told that Mick had gone away. No-one knew where, and although I combed the streets, and Brook Vale, it was hopeless. I checked the local council yards and police stations in case he'd been involved in an accident, but I never saw him again.

I don't remember crying over his loss, well, big boys don't, do they? However, I often think of him coming to my aid as the

Apaches began to close in, looking at me with unconcealed pleasure as I patted him on the head.

Faithful old Mick. Who are you running with now?

Chapter 5

Bonfire night is remembered as a time of great excitement. For weeks prior to November 5th, our gang endeavoured to collect every scrap of burnable material we could lay our hands on. Most people seized the opportunity to clear their homes of junk: old three piece suites, tables, beds, and garden prunings. I once removed hundreds of old newspapers from a house, some of which I clearly recall dated as far back as the 1870's. I could cry when I think what happened to them. Even today people still take the opportunity to get rid of rubbish this way.

Having accumulated all the 'bommy' wood, the next step was to find somewhere to store it, preferably somewhere dry and safe to prevent rival gangs from making off with it. Even though 'bommy' wood was plentiful in the area on the first bonfire night after the war, we still used to take great delight in raiding each others stores. Raiding was a traditional part of the game and was accepted as such. Now and then our spies would uncover news of a possible raid on our store and we would lie in wait watching the attackers advancing, then pounce. Usually a pitched battle ensued but after the shock of walking into an ambush it was enough to make them flee in terror. A debris of arrows and stones were strewn in their wake!

We often raided many opposing bommy stores and after a battle that could last an hour or more, return to our own territory dragging our spoils behind us. The greeting cheers of the guards we left behind had a magical healing effect on our cuts and bruises. It said much for our defensive capabilities that we were very rarely raided. If we were, it was usually from a distance with fire arrows, in the vain hope of setting fire to our store. As ours was piled into an old bombed out shop on Rawson Road, later to become a newsagent, only a frontal attack stood any chance of success.

Once though, our impregnable fortress was in danger of being over-run and the only way to save it was a full scale counter-charge. We managed to repulse the raiders but in doing so, myself and my faithful lieutenant, Jimmy Clandillon, were captured and taken back to the enemy's lair at the back of the houses in Sandy Road. We were threatened with the usual tortures, but Jimmy and I were made of sterner stuff and didn't crack under their threats.

"You'd better talk," threatened Tony Williams, their leader, " 'cos if you don't, we're going to tie you up and leave you here all night and the rats will eat your feet!" I couldn't stand rats and this caused me to blanch a little, but I put on a brave face.

"Yeah? Well, that won't worry us!" I said defiantly. "Rats don't scare us, do they, Jimmy?" Jimmy, looking rather pale in the thickening light, puffed out his chest and sneered.

"Do your worst!" he said with equal bravado. "We won't talk!"

Nevertheless, the mental picture of a rat nibbling on my big toe and eying my little toe for dessert did nothing to bolster my confidence. "There's a quicker way to sort this out," I said to Tony, hoping I sounded braver than I felt.

"Oh yeah, and what might that be?" he said in a voice that sounded like someone who held all the aces, and then some.

"As leader of our gang, I'll fight the leader of your gang," I said, knowing full well it was him, "and the winner will get a ransom of as much bommy wood that they can take away". I saw a film once when Randolph Scott said the same to Cochise, to guarantee the safety of the wagon train. In my case I'd suggested the fight so I could get home before it went dark! His gang huddled in a group for a few moments then Tony came back and after weighing me up, no doubt noting my slight physique, nodded.

"It's a deal", he said. Encouraged by the yells of the onlookers, we fought to a standstill. We both had cuts and bloodied faces and worst of all scraped knees that stung. In the end it was declared a draw and we were released. We were still jeered at as we made our way out of the field and then we started throwing stones at each other. I was gratified to hear someone yell out in pain as one of my missiles struck home.

"Hey, Tony!", I shouted as we neared the road.

"What?" he yelled back.

"I'll see you in school tomorrow".

His voice was barely audible but clear enough.

"Okay Charlie. See ya'".

I suppose the biggest bommy in the district was that of the Mayor of Crosby. On the great night he ambled up, put a torch to it and retired, as though following the instructions on a firework. It was always built on spacious, derelict areas and therefore posed no threat to surrounding properties. Ours was erected on the nearest available bombed site, regardless of where that was. However, if it was dangerous the Fire Brigade came clanging down the road and hosed it into submission, then retreated accompanied by cat calls and the raising of many fingers. To see this happen was heartbreaking. Many weeks of work doused with water, disappearing in a cloud of ash and hissing steam.

When this occurred we would run pell mell to our enemies of the day previous and join theirs. We were always welcomed, as they would have been to ours had their bommy suffered a similar fate. All the enmity and animosity of the past weeks would be forgotten. Friends and foe would watch the sparks from the fire leap into the air and flit like glow worms across the night sky.

But to return to the Mayors bommy, it always appeared massive and I suppose it was, for he had a virtual army collecting for it. The council! Trees were felled, derelict houses were cleared of timber and flammable materials were brought in from all over the place and transported and stored at the site. The desire to raid this cache of bommy wood became obsessive. To raid it with any degree of success was to reach the pinnacle of fame in the eyes of rival gangs and a place in history was assured!

I take pride in recording that I led raids on three occasions and was never thwarted. It was always well guarded and often ended in hand to hand fighting. I did sometimes wonder if it was worth all the effort, because we had to drag our spoils across the tip, over Brook Vale bridge and up Cambridge Road, before we reached the safety of our own store. A trek of over half a mile! In the end, though, we knew we could live off the prestige for the next twelve months.

I saved all the pennies and ha'pennies I could lay my hands on in order to buy fireworks. I ran the usual errands and brushed leaves from paths, but it was a slow and painful task trying to earn enough to buy a few bangers. When I managed to buy a couple I would run home and hide them in a safe place. Some children arrived on the night with an impressive assortment and I would look on in wonder, and with a little envy, as I patted the half dozen or so in my pocket. I was blissfully unaware how stupid I was keeping them there!

It always seemed to be raining on bommy night and we would stare sadly at our soaking heap and speculate on its success as the crowds began to gather. There was never any shortage of help and often a kind parent would appear bearing a can of paraffin. Once the flames became established the rain was a beaten contestant and soon the whole pyramid became engulfed. Arm chairs and settees, which had been somebody's pride and joy, succumbed quickly and springs stuck out at crazy angles. Old pieces of lino' melted and a black tar-like substance which ran onto the timbers gave the flames fresh impetus.

Deep orange, blue, green and yellow flames, all gave a myriad of colour from the different materials being consumed. On top, the Guy gave a stupid grin as he toppled into the inferno and people cheered at his demise. The more adventurous edged nearer, only to scatter squealing as the wind fanned the flames in their direction, the crowd laughing at their misfortune.

Children danced and cavorted in delight as Rip-Raps, Bangers, Roman candles and various coloured 'rains' cascaded around them. Their force was soon spent and the fireworks died, their carcasses spluttering defiantly. An occasional rocket might 'whoosh' into the sky and explode in a waterfall of glistening stars, bringing 'oohs' and 'ahs' from the watching crowd. We strutted around proudly, for it was we who had instigated these few hours of excitement.

Later, as the fire reduced in intensity and the flames were calmed through lack of fuel, most people drifted away. This was the time I liked best, for in the heap of smouldering embers were my potatoes. There was no such thing as cooking foil to keep them clean or indeed to keep them visible. After some speculative poking about in the ashes I would retrieve them black and usually incinerated, but they tasted delicious and even the charcoal-like skin was devoured.

On bommy night I was allowed to stay out until 11 O' Clock. This was very much an exception to the rule and we sat around the remains of our endeavours, telling ghost stories, arms and legs mottled with the heat. We were all a little sad that it was all over for another year, but content enough to sit poking at the dying fire, like prodding a fallen enemy to see if it wasstill alive.

The following morning saw me running back to the site. It would still be smouldering and the warmth would penetrate the soles of my goloshes as I poked about in the ashes. I could guarantee finding some coppers that had dropped from the dark recess of an old armchair. On top of that there was always the scrap to salvage and weigh in later. Many pairs of brass hinges and locks have often been my reward.

These days I have a small bommy in the garden for my own children. We have fireworks (a lot more than half a dozen!) and jacket potatoes, in foil, of course. I'm not sure about bommy night anymore. I hope I don't sound like an old grouch, but whereas we would toss the odd banger around, there was never any malice in it, and no intention to harm.

Today, with fireworks becoming more powerful and more dangerous, organised displays are far safer. I'm afraid I'd like the public sale of them banned. The risk far outweighs any fun that's had and maybe it's time to let Guy Fawkes topple into the flames for the last time.

Chapter 6

I looked over to where Bill was flapping his arms in an attempt to increase his circulation and wondered, not for the first time, if we should call it a day. It was early February in 1946 and we had been ferreting since first light without success. Due to our recent inactivity we had allowed the cold to creep into our bones and now we were beginning to feel miserable. It was cold, really cold. The snow, which had frozen overnight, crunched and crackled with each step I took. The air felt fresh and clean and when I breathed, steamy clouds swirled around my head. The countryside around looked as if it had been freshly laundered and snow hung from the branches of bushes like delicate lace filigree. We had spent most of the morning in and around Altcar Camp and it had looked promising at first, but although there were plenty of tracks criss-crossing the ranges, we hadn't flushed out a single rabbit.

After a while, we made our way towards the River Alt and could see the masts of sailing vessels swaying to and fro above the high bank. Overhead, ink-black crows flapped laboriously in the direction of the tall trees near the camp entrance, cawing their disapproval at the snow which had fallen overnight. Away to the right, and in the lee of the sand hills, fields dipped and rolled like a heavy sea swell in the direction of Hall Road. The river flowed sluggishly through the reed beds and I was surprised to see that it had not frozen over completely. A yard from either bank the water had been stilled by platforms of blue, grey ice, but down the centre, unhindered by any restrictions, it tumbled and swirled triumphantly toward the sea.

As I scrambled to the top of a high bank, a pair of mallards suddenly took flight a few feet from me, flapping and squawking wildly. Their alarm was nothing to the terror they instilled in me and I sat on the scrub with my heart pounding, as they flew low and fast towards bushes surrounding an iced-over pond about a hundred yards away. Sun rays slanted to earth through breaks in the snow-laden clouds, enveloping the whole scene in an orangey glow. It was as though an artist had suddenly decided to introduce colour to his canvass. We sat on a partly buried log to catch our breath and re-assess the situation.

"There's not a lot happening today, is there, Bill?" I said flatly. "I think we should call it a day and maybe try our luck on the way home."

"I think you're right," Bill agreed. "We could try further over toward Sniggery Wood. I had some luck there last time," he added optimistically.

"Okay. We'll give it one more go." I stood up and brushed the particles of snow from my coat. In a field to our left, plovers scratched and scraped in the snow for tit-bits. Overhead, seagulls cackled and screeched, gracefully gliding down to a stop and dropping the last few inches to earth. With a wag of tails and a rouse of feathers, they nestled into a snowy blanket. Indifferent to their presence, the plovers stoicly pranced around, busy with their own task.

The wind had increased, but at least the trees would afford some protection from the wind chill. Our actions caused the more alert gulls to lift their heads and monitor our movements, but as we were moving away from them and posed no threat, they resumed their position, heads tucked beneath a wing, the wind ruffling their feathers like a lady's fan.

The trees at the edge of Sniggery Wood bent before the force of the north-west wind as though digging their heels in to defy the elements. Branches flailed the air in helpless confusion and the last of the leaves released their grip and were whipped away into obscurity. The grass, blackened by frost and snow the night previous, had lost its vitality and decided to remain dormant until spring. What remained of Sniggery Sidings was visible from where we stood, a stark reminder of when the area was a transit camp for men being transported to the Flanders poppy fields during the First World War. A brook, gurgling and tumbling over rocks below where I stood, seemed as lively as ever, and roused me from my reverie.

Nearby, a few birds took to the air only to be swept away like kites out of control and only continued on their chosen course by flying close to the ground, where the winds ferocity was tamed by the brush and scrub dotted about. In the distance the snow covered roofs of nearby Little Crosby stood out in stark contrast against the threatening black skies and smoke from cottage chimneys spiralled upward momentarily, before being whipped away by the wind.

There were a number of 'live' warrens in the surrounding area but we made for the one that Bill had tried before and judging by the tracks around the entrance, it was obvious that it was a very active warren. We surveyed the entrances and decided to give it one last try. I netted all the holes but one and into this we placed Jenny. Jenny was Bill's ferret and she snuffled in protest as she was pulled from the bag, her red eyes blinking in the sudden light.

For a moment or two she sat sniffing at the entrance, then in her rolling gait shuffled into the darkness. We waited, glancing at the netted holes expecting to see one bulge with a startled rabbit but for a full five minutes we heard nothing. A ship's horn boomed a warning from the river and was immediately answered by a shrill and more distant one. It was becoming foggy and would soon turn into a 'peasouper'. We were about to call Jenny out, when we heard muffled squealing and knew at once she had caught a rabbit in a blind corner.

The grunting of Jenny and the thumping and growling of the rabbit became more distinct and it dawned on me that she was literally pulling one out. Soon Jenny's yellow rump came into view and we tried to grab her but the hole was a narrow one with little room to spare around her fat body. Gradually, she edged out of the hole and I noted with disgust that she had the rabbit by the nose and mouth and was using her enormous strength to drag her out. With an effort, we pulled both the rabbit and Jenny clear of the hole. Jenny, her mouth covered in soil and blood, licked her lips and protested loudly as she was thrust into the bag. I took the rabbit and hit it on the back of the neck, killing it quickly. I was filled with compassion for that unfortunate creature. It is hard to imagine it's terror as it found itself cornered by an opponent who knew only how to kill.

One ear had been completely torn off. It's rump had been ripped and bitten as it had turned it's back to kick out with its powerful back legs. Already in terrible pain it had felt the ferret gripping its nose and dragging it out of the hole. I looked down at the poor unfortunate rabbit with its badly mutilated face and wondered how the other occupants of the warren would be feeling tonight at this loss. I had been ferreting for many years and normally a rabbit that bolts into a net is dispatched quickly, but this 'kill' filled me with revulsion and disgust. Even though Jenny had done the job she had been bred and trained for, I couldn't help the feeling of loathing that came over me when I looked at her. I knew as surely as spring followed winter, I would never go ferreting again.

Chapter 7

When I was a young lad I used to spend a lot of my time trying to get enough coppers together for the 'Pictures'. My parents didn't have money for me to 'fritter' away on the movies, so I had to earn it myself. Consequently, I rarely dawdled after the school bell sounded. Before the clapper came to rest, I was off and running and in minutes was passing the Sandown Hotel on Sandy Road and still going strong!

A quick change into some old shorts and before you could say 'Durrango Kid', I was off to the tip to search among the rubbish for scrap and anything of value. It was normally quiet at that time of the day. The 'raggies' had long since departed to 'weigh in' and only a few people wandered around looking for odds and ends: bicycle parts to mend an old relic, pram wheels to make a cart and even discarded radio sets, which, with a bit of tinkering and possibly a new valve, could be persuaded to tune in to the sounds of 'Itma' or, my favourite, 'Dick Barton,- Special Agent'.

In those balmy days shortly after the war it was very much a case of make do and mend. I've knocked many an old bike together from bits I found poking around in the rubbish. It may have wobbled a little, it may have had a tendency to suddenly stop and send you curving gracefully over the handlebars, but that didn't matter. It was the acheivment of making a bicycle out of oddments that was satisfying. Usually, the tip provided me with what I needed. It may not turn up that day, but it would eventually come to light. I used to rake among the rubbish for hours, throwing likely oddments to one side for sorting, until I had gathered together all I could carry. Jam Jars were much sought after and usually a scramble developed to claim the sticky container as it tumbled from the jaws of a bin wagon. A one pound jar fetched a ha'penny and a two pound one, a penny. Lemonade bottles were a treat to find, but it was a tricky operation going from shop to shop with different brands trying to get the refund on them. I've chilled from many a cold stare as shop owners sorted through them.

"That's not mine. Nor that. Are you sure you got them here?"

"Oh yes", I would answer, as straight faced as I could, "my sister bought them last week".

One flaw with collecting lemonade bottles, especially those I had rescued from the tip, was that you had to be careful when you washed them as very often the labels fell off, and with no gum to stick them back on, it rendered them useless. I did have limited success with a mixture of flour and water , but it was dodgy as they had to pass the shop-keepers close scrutiny.

Jam-jars, on the other hand, could be scrubbed with little effort and, having washed them, I would load my old pram and take them to Arthur Watt's Scrap Yard on Bridge Road. Normally, a queue of handcarts waited to unload at the scales, and one or two like myself, with a loaded pram! Over to one side the sorters were separating and weighing the different metals before throwing them onto the growing heaps. Very often there was a look of disappointment on the `raggies' faces when they returned from the office. Payments for their scrap rarely came up to expectations. In the shed men were busy baling rags and woollens ready for shipment. The place was alive, and not just with people! My jars were handed over and inspected for cracks or chipped edges. His men would count them, then stack them at the rear of the yard. The stacked jars were a sight to see, a huge glass pyramid that distorted the figures of the stackers as they moved around the back of the pile. It never entered my head to question why only jam jars and no other glass containers were in such demand. I was content to take advantage of the money to be earned in this way and clutching the pennies counted into my hand, pushed them deep into my pocket.

Having experienced the empty feeling that comes over you

when your last precious coin has rolled into a gutter and fell down a grid, I rarely missed an opportunity to rake through the leafy sludge that was spewed from the gully sucking lorries. Occasionally a threepenny 'joey' or, if you were very lucky, a silver sixpence would come to light. By whatever means, come saturday morning I had accumulated my matinee money and have enough left for little treats on my way to school, and occasionally, I could spare a copper for the 'waifs and strays' fund in school!

I rarely had money to spend any other day of the week, but on Mondays, I was a millionaire! My habit was to leave early and walk down Sandy Road, past Seaforth Barracks, toward Seaforth LMS Station. On the corner of Green Lane stood Myers' pawnshop. The three brass balls hanging outside were peeled and dented and in need of attention, but on a Monday it was the most popular shop in Seaforth! Clogs and golloshers hung outside, strung up like bunches of onions. I often had to wear clogs and although heavy looking they were surprisingly comfortable, and certainly substantial! However, after constant wear, the hooped iron on the sole became as sharp as a razor and many a ball I've burst going into a tackle! Eventually, players wearing clogs were banned and, as buying footie boots was out of the question, I played a lot of football in goloshes or 'pumps'. It took a certain amount of skill to tackle someone who was wearing football boots and emerge unscathed!

Normally, a small queue of women hugging bundles of clothes or bedding, stood chatting, waiting to be admitted into the side entrance to haggle for a few extra shillings that would help ease their financial worries until the end of the week. It was not unusual, on a Monday morning, to see Mrs Povey pushing an ancient pram loaded with bedding and bundles to join the queue of women talking quietly together. It was an equally common sight to see her push the whole lot back on Friday! It was a mystery to me what the family slept on during the rest of the week! A friend of mine who went to work there after leaving school, watched as his mother handed her pledges over the counter, then passed the whole lot back out to her through a side window!

At the end of Sandy Road, the last shop in a row of small and twisted shops stood Ross's and, as the legend above the door stated:

"THE BEST FOR FRUIT AND VEG".

The stall immediately to the left of the entrance was heaped with bruised apples and pears for customers who wanted a pennyworth of 'fades', but tucked just behind the door, was a small hooped barrel fitted with a wooden lid and lined with grease proof paper. It contained the most delicious peanut butter.

"Yis, luv?" asked a rosy cheeked lady in a dull green overall.

"Can I have a portion of peanut butter, please?" She would sniff at me imperiously.

"That'll be a penny," and throwing my penny into a drawer, scoop out a generous portion of the brown mixture into a square of newspaper and hand it to me. As the day wore on I found it necessary to reinforce this with several more pieces of paper to prevent the grease from seeping through. As it was always too big for my pocket, no precise weighing in those days, the precious parcel went inside my shirt where I could scoop at it all day through a specially prepared hole. Schoolboys hands are notoriously grubby things and mine were no exception, but on Mondays I sported a glorious white forefinger! When I look along Supermarket shelves today, I can see jars and jars of peanut butter with titles like 'Smooth and Crunchy' and even 'Super Crunchy'. My peanut butter on the other hand was neither 'factory fresh' or fortified with 'vitamins', but it was much more satisfying.

Willie the Milkman, whistling soundlessly, urged his pony and trap up Seaforth Road towards the dairy, his early round completed. A couple of years previous I had stood looking at some of Willies cows lying dead in the road after an air-raid on the district. They were never replaced and I supposed he was supplied with milk by local farmers. Five minutes to Nine and across the road to Dean's cake shop. Barmcakes were two for a penny and right out of the oven! On winter mornings I used to eat the hot doughy centres then burrow my hands inside them and wear them like gloves. It was only later, when they had cooled, that I ate the crispy shell. Today that would be looked upon as crass and silly, but in those days nobody gave me a second glance or if they did I was totally unaware of it!

The shops have long since gone. Their place is now occupied by a footbridge and car park, although I cannot honestly say the environment has been improved by their destruction. Dean's cake shop escaped the developers scythe and I'm happy to say it still remains and has so far managed to fend off the embracing arm of the bigger and more powerful bakeries.

I bought some barmcakes from Deans recently, but alas, I can't get my hands inside them anymore! I tried, just to see, and received one or two sidelong glances from passers-by and more than my fair share of the pavement! It proves one thing, though. We never really grow up, do we?

Chapter 8

I raced around to the back of the house to get my football kit and as I turned into the kitchen my eyes fell upon the bottle warming on the hearth by the fire. I froze, but it was too late. I tried to retrace my steps but my mams voice stopped me in my tracks.

"Just the fellow I've been waiting for. Stay right where you are!" Escape was impossible. My first mistake was not looking through the window before I came in. It was Friday and I should have known better. On alternate Fridays, my mam used to torture us with Castor Oil and Syrup Of Figs. 'To keep you regular' she used to say. I don't know if it kept me regular or not, but I can say with certainty that I stayed close to home the following day!

This was before the large selection of breakfast cereals that people enjoy today were available and words like "ruffage" became part of my vocabulary. Mind you, having tasted one or two of today's products, I am not impressed. It was rather like chomping my way through a bale of hay! On reflection, I think the bale of hay just edged it, on taste! However, I desperately needed to get out of my present predicament because my turn to 'open wide' loomed closer.

"Mam, I can't stop! We've got this football match at five and . . ." but my mam was ahead of me and a spoon was pushed-firmly into my mouth, stifling the possibility of further conversation. I am not referring to the dainty teaspoon that you swirl gently around a teacup, or the spoon that you scoop up succulent pieces of fruit or pie with. Oh, no. This 'medicine' spoon was like a soup ladle! The oily liquid slid down my throat causing me to gag and I felt as though I'd just had an oil change. "There now," my mam would say, "that'll do you good". I questioned the wisdom of her statement, though not out loud. How can something that makes you feel sick and contorted your insides as though you'd been disembowelled, do you good?

Far and away the worst form of torture that my mam indulged in regularly, was to scalp us with a Derback comb or, as she called it, 'a fine toothed comb'. The object of the excersise was to 'seek out and destroy' nits. The very mention of their name caused people to breathe in sharply. Parents in the immediate vicinity drew their offspring closer to their skirts. Oh, the shame of having nits! And worse still, coming home from school with a note from the nurse! It was for that very reason my mam introduced us all to 'the fine toothed comb'.

"You're next!" she would announce and look directly at her chosen victim. The remainder of the family tried to vacate the room adopting various methods of subterfuge, but my mam kept a wary eye on us all. To someone who hasn't experienced the horrors of it I can only liken it to a sadistic gardener combing your scalp with lawn rake! Even now, years later, I break out in a cold sweat when the barber shouts "Next!"

My mam also had this undying faith in Goose grease! Luckily, we could only afford goose once a year and, of course, that was at Christmas time. She believed that rubbed liberally on your chest, it contained magical powers to keep the cold out, the heat in and germs at bay. I don't know about germs, but it kept my friends at arms length, assured me of a desk all to myself at school and caused me to walk like the Tin Man in the 'Wizard Of Oz'.

At night before going to bed, my mam slapped it on. I couldn't believe a goose had that much grease in it and she seemed to have an endless supply! I suspected her of topping it up with some other concoction, to make it go further. When we played hide and seek, my break for freedom was usually short lived. I left a vapour trail in my wake which was easily followed, even by someone suffering from a heavy cold, and in no time I was in the 'bin'!

Mick, my dog, was never very far from my side, but when my

mam had given me the grease treatment, he would sniff the air appreciatively and lick his lips in anticipation! There was an extra bounce in his step because he thought I was carrying the remains of the goose in my pocket and at any moment I was going to fling him a leg! It was understandable really because every now and then fumes from my jumper would assail my nostrils and even I had to admit, I smelt worse than a butchers apron! My only true friend during my 'greasy' period was Vicky who showed unyielding loyalty toward me when no-one else did! Eventually, the smelly goo was used up and my friends began to call again, tentatively at first, then with growing confidence!

Like all young boys I sustained many cuts and bruises during my escapades and I can honestly say they never bothered me or stopped me from playing out. On the really deep cuts, a plaster to hold it together was fine, and on grazes a cold flannel, usually did the trick. What did bother me, though, was if my mam knew about them. I would go to any lengths to prevent her from seeing any injury, no matter how slight, because that meant only one thing, one of her favourite remedy's, Iodine! How anyone could inflict iodine on another human being is beyond me, but my mam did, and with gusto!

"It'll only sting for a minute" she used to say. Which was true, but what an agonizing minute! It used to feel like someone had tied a rip-rap to my leg!

I must have suffered a vitamin deficiency when I was growing up because I went through a period when I never seemed to be without a boil or two, somewhere on my person. My mam would get me between her knees and do her best to, as she put it 'squeeze out the core'. Applying steady pressure, using her thumbs she would knead and press for ages. It could prove quite painful but very often her attempts had to be aborted because it was 'deep seated'! When that happened my mam produced her secret weapon, the bread and sugar poultice. And it used to work a treat! As a 'drawing' agent it had no equal.

That is, until my mam discovered 'Kaolin Poultice' She thought that it might be an improvement on the bread and sugar poultices and bought a tin from the chemists. It had a consistency similar to molten lava and had the same effect when it came in contact with the skin!

I recall a time when I sustained a nasty injury playing football and I ignored it. Soon, it became infected. When I realised that dock leaves were not going to do the trick it filled me with dismay. I knew what was going to happen as soon as my mam saw it! One of the draw-backs of wearing short trousers was that it was impossible to hide any injury on the legs. As I feared, she homed in on my leg like radar and spotting my red, angry looking shin, sprang into action. I sat in the chair a helpless captive and watched the 'tin' warming on the stove. It plopped once or twice like boiling mud and when my mam thought it was right, she spread a liberal coating on a piece of lint. Had she tested it to make sure it was reasonably warm and lowered it gently onto my leg, all might have been well. However, she was more used to the bread and sugar jobs, so she just flopped it on! If you were to visit my old address in Sandringham Road and look to the ceiling in the kitchen, there may still be one or two small indentations in the plasterwork where I hit it! I don't remember much else, apart from the excruciating pain. Eventually, I had to go to Waterloo Hospital as an out-patient and receive penicillin injections!

Most of the old remedy's really were successful in relieving pain and suffering, buf there was one that not only inflicted pain but also acute embarrassment! I refer to the moment my mam thought my face looked grubby and decided to do something about it. It was only when I saw her fiddling about in her handbag that I realised what was coming. The `spit wet' hanky! The location didn't save me either. Whether we were walking down the street or were slap bang in the middle of a large store, it didn't matter, you were going to get the 'spit wet' hanky! Very often it came without warning. There I was enjoying a rare day out in town, looking forward to an ice cream, when suddenly I was attacked by my mam. And it was always the same.

"Come here you. I can't go anywhere without you making a show of me! How did you get so dirty?"

At the same time as I was being admonished, for something I wasn't aware of in the first place, my mam would grab me by the hair and yank my head back. Then it came. The spit wet hanky to scrub my face with! The only defensive action I used to take was to screw my eyes tight shut and purse my lips tight. Believe me, when my mam had you by the hair, there was no other option left open to you! It took the shine off the rest of the day but put a shine on my face! Come to think of it, I can't recall seeing any youngsters being given the 'hanky' treatment for years! They can thank their lucky stars that someone invented Wet Wipes. Apart from it being far more hygienic it is also far less embarrassing, especially when you're about fourteen!

Chapter 9

"It's getting late, Bill. I think we'd better get organised for the night, don't you?" Bill was a mate of mine and we seized every opportunity to go shooting that came our way: marsh flats, farmers fields, anywhere we could get permission, and quite a few places we didn't! As spring was turning into summer we had taken the long and tedious journey to Loggerheads, about five miles past Ruthin in North Wales. To say we travelled light would be an understatement. All we carried were our guns, plus ammunition of course, a frying pan, two forks and a pound of butter, all comfortably stowed in one small pack. We intended to live on what nature would provide and we were good at it. Daniel Boone could teach us nothing and even Buffalo Bill would have arched an approving eyebrow.

Stepping from the bus with a cheery "Yakki Dar" to the conductor, whatever that might mean, and nothing much judging by his expression, we headed into the trees at the bottom of the escarpment, a granite formation rising sheer to our right. On ledges where wind-borne soil had collected, small stunted shrubs and patches of fescue grasses grew; this was nature's way of giving a normally grey face a touch of make-up. Two hundred yards away from the cliff face, a stream hastened toward the River Clwyd, sometimes noisily as it rushed pell mell over boulders, at others silently, swirling in deep, dark stretches. Sandwiched between cliff and river were thick woods. There were few Pine trees, but Elm, Oak, Mountain Ash and many others were in abundance. Huge roots protruding above the ground, criss-crossed in open areas, like fingers seeking a fresh hold on mother earth. In the distance Moel Famau and Moel Arthur showed darkly against the evening sky.

The whole scene of cliff, river and woods followed in a two mile semi-circle, separating occasionally, but coming together further on in a joyous mixture of colour and noise. The cliff itself diminished in height until it feathered to a grassy plain. An enormous wedge of rock had pushed up from the earth millions of years ago, reaching its highest point where we entered, at about two hundred feet.

It was nearing dusk when we arrived at a suitable place to make camp. We hadn't brought a tent as we intended to make a protective covering out of branches and brushwood. It didn't take us long to collect what we needed and in no time had erected a shelter for the night. With a foot thick mattress of leaves and dried grass on the floor, we were set for whatever nature might send our way, provided she wasn't too hard on us!

It took me some time to fall asleep that first night and I lay there listening to the sounds of the night. All the Crickets in the area seemed to have gathered outside our shelter, for no other purpose than to keep us awake all night. Lambs, following their mothers and nuzzling for a feed, bleated piteously and sounded remarkably like little babies. The yap of a fox sounded, calling to its mate as they closed in on some unsuspecting prey. A slap of wings echoed noisily as a night bird took to the air, startled from its roost and scores of different insects chattered and leaves rustled, as night things went about their business. After a while the cacophony of sounds eased and I slept.

It was early morning sunlight that prompted my eyes to open to the world. It was a beautiful morning. The woods had come alive, each creature greeting the new day in its own way. After a quick breakfast we set off to explore, entering the woods at the lower end of the valley, near to the river. As morning progressed rapidly into mid- afternoon we were still creeping and stalking through sparse patches of scrub looking for rabbits.

Suddenly a grey squirrel ran up the trunk of a tree and along a branch, intent on leaping to the cliff face. As it leapt, Bill shot it in mid flight. It tumbled down and dropped into a ditch filled with rocks and brambles.

"Hold my gun, Charl, I'll go and get it", he said excitedly. To us, shooting grey squirrels was justifiable as they were considered a pest in most areas they populated. Bill was searching among the rocks with the aid of a stick when he gave a cry of pain and clutched at his leg. I saw at once the reason for his alarm. Slithering through the rocks, with surprising speed, was an adder. Bill scrambled out of the ditch white faced and cursing. He sat on a boulder to roll up his trouser leg and midway between his ankle and calf were two little puncture marks about half an inch apart.

Although adder bites can make you extremely ill for a day or so, they are very rarely fatal. However, we didn't know this at the time and I had visions of Bill lying semi-conscious, his leg a bloated, ugly thing asking in a barely audible voice, for a drink of water. It was a bit like something from the movies. I was John Wayne and Bill was William Holden.

"There's nothing else for it, Bill", I said sadly, "the poison has to come out".

"I know," he nodded miserably. I took out my knife and held it over a burning match, then tried to nick across the punctures. Bill would have none of it and shouted, quite unreasonably, I thought.

"You can sod off with that knife!" As he was reluctant to co-operate with that particular remedy, I bent down and tried to suck at the wound. For my trouble, I got nothing but a nasty taste in my mouth, and a sore back from Bill pummelling on it!

The idea came to me so quickly that it startled Bill as I stood up. Removing a cartridge from my belt, I opened the top and poured out the shot. Then probed at the cardboard wad that separated the powder from the load.

"What are you going to do with that thing?" Bill demanded, a look of terror on his face.

"It's your only chance", I said soothingly. "It will only take a second and It'll burn out the poison and seal the wound from infection. Trust me, you'll see, it'll work fine. Have I ever let you down?"

Reluctantly, he admitted I hadn't and with a tremor in his voice he agreed to let me try.   I sprinkled the black powder onto his leg, about half a thimble full, making sure that the area around the bite was covered in a nice even layer. Next I struck a match and selected a long twiggy taper and lit it.

"Now turn your face away, Bill, then you won't know when I'm going to do it, okay?" I was sounding more like the 'Duke' by the minute!

Bill's pale face nodded at me then he turned to one side. Reaching at arms length I touched the powder with the taper. So much happened in the few seconds that followed that it's difficult to recall in detail. There was a flash of brilliant colour, and ballooning lazily upwards, a mushroom of black smoke. The smell of burnt powder mixed with singed flesh was over-powering and it took a while to get my breath. When the smoke cleared Bill wasn't where he should have been. 'Crikey' thought, 'I've blown him to pieces' and began frantically searching the surrounding area for fragments of clothing and charred flesh.

I began to panic and in desperation looked about me. It was then that I heard, rather than saw, a lone figure bounding down the hill and crashing through the undergrowth like a bull elephant. The thing that stands out vividly, even to this day, is how like one he sounded, too. With some relief I saw it was Bill and snatching up the guns, gave chase. I caught up with him as we reached camp. He was sitting on the floor clutching his leg and moaning as he rocked back and forth.   "What's wrong, Bill?" I asked hesitantly. He looked up at me with tears in his eyes.

"What's wrong? What's wrong?" he shouted, quite beside himself. "You stupid bugger, look at my bloody leg!"

I looked and managed to stem the flow of hysterical laughter I knew was just beneath the surface. Where there had been two small punctures, there was one large one about the size of a shilling and a very angry looking red and black burn surrounding it.

"Well, it must have done some good", I answered, pulling the guns out of his reach, "look how you could run on it!"

He continued to rock and moan and in moments of calm fix me with a venomous glare. I was hurt and bemused by his show of ingratitude. Here was I, the victim of his rebuke and I probably saved his life. Later, his leg began to swell alarmingly and any thoughts of continuing the camp were abandoned. So I packed our gear and with Bill leaning on me for support, we made our way to rendezvous with the bus.

When we arrived back in Liverpool some hours later, we went straight to the hospital. The doctor on duty in Casualty widened his eyes in horror when I told him what had happened and what measures had been taken. He looked at me for some time, then, like someone emerging from an hypnotic trance, shook his head and bent to the task of what he called 'repairing the damage.'

The outcome was that Bill was detained in hospital and remained there for a week while he underwent a course of penicillin injections, to prevent blood poisoning, they said. This struck me as odd because that's what I thought I'd done when I ignited the gunpowder! I saw Bill years later.

"I've still got the scar "he said, pulling his trouser leg up.

"The scar!" I said, laughing, "you're lucky you still have the leg!"

Chapter 10

I sat up in bed rubbing the sleep from my eyes feeling strangely happy. With an effort I tried to unscramble my thoughts into something comprehensible. Of course! Today was Gala Day. I dressed hurriedly and half an hour and a jam butty later, I was calling for my friends. Although the war years had stifled 'people's appetites' for enjoyment, the dark, oppressive cloud of deprivation was slowly lifting and gradually their taste buds were being re-awakened. It could be said that Gala Day was a 'tasty starter'.

Many local borough committees began to re-introduce galas or carnivals in order to raise money, the proceeds of which went to assist local hospitals and charities. It was an annual event and the procession, starting at Waterloo Town Hall, snaked its way around the major roads of the borough. People came in droves to admire the many marvellous floats and costumes of those who flanked the slow moving parade, rattling collection boxes. Weeks before Gala Day, dedicated folk braved the elements and worked hard to get everything ready.

Fierce looking pirates, beautiful, eastern princesses, cowboys and clowns. Indians wearing striking war-paint and feathered head-dresses ran about whooping and threatening the crowds with tomahawks, and they in turn recoiled in mock horror, giggling. The whole carnival route was alive with colour, shouting, and peals of laughter. Shire horses were decked out in their finest ribbons and rosettes with brasses that gleamed so bright you could comb your hair in them.

It was traditional in these events to choose a Gala Queen. Young ladies who varied in age, from fourteen to nineteen. Hopeful candidates were interviewed by a committee and eventually, by a process of elimination, a gala queen was selected for the June procession. On Gala Day she was normally driven around the chosen route in an open, horse drawn carriage, but occasionally she would sit majestically on a golden throne mounted on the back of a specially prepared lorry, smiling her 'regal' smile and waving in a 'majestic' fashion. Her ladies in waiting, the runners up, sat by her feet, a fixed though disappointed smile on their faces.

When the Queen passed, for reasons I've never been able to fathom, the crowds lining the street became quiet and subdued, almost reverent. In hushed tones they uttered things like "isn't she lovely" and hoisting small children on their shoulders would point saying, "Look, it's the Queen". As the various floats passed by, people lining the road threw pennies and ha'pennies onto the flatbed lorries which were gathered up by helpers. Some floats were manned by people reaching out with fishing nets attached to long canes in an attempt to catch the coins as they were thrown. I liked to stand and watch from the corner of Kinross Road and Crosby Road and very often a coin would fall short of the net and clatter to the ground. These were retrieved and thrown onto the back of the lorry, at least most of them were!

All the organised galas were wonderful affairs, but I think the one held in Crosby was generally accepted as being the best. After the parade, which lasted about half an hour, the procession finally congregated at a large grassed field near the beach at Seaforth, adjacent to Potter's Barn.

Preparations for the gala site had started a week earlier. The perimeter was fenced and the gates erected. Next, the arena was built for the displays and a grandstand for the V.I.Ps. Toward the end of the week the fun-fair would arrive and in a short time tents, side stalls and all manner of attractions began to be erected. We were often hired by the fairground boss to fetch and carry and help lay out the various stalls. Our reward was normally a 'two bob bit' and the odd glass of lemonade. When I added this to what I'd already earned on various errands, and 'weighing in' scrap metal I'd collected, a good night at the fair was assured. Finally, the 'waltzer' and a few other rides were added and men strung long lines of coloured lights across the gaily painted boards. Before long all was ready for the gay and exciting day.

The Mayor and other dignitaries, together with the Gala Queen, took up seats in the centre of the stand. The rest were taken up by people who were prepared to pay for the comfort of the stand rather than be pushed and jostled at the barriers. As the week wore on the displays in the arena became less attractive and there was always room around the perimeter. The first day, though, was special and was always exciting.

Police motor cycle teams performed stunts of daring and could form human pyramids while on the move or ride through blazing fire hoops. I used to love the wrestling and still remember a local favourite, Jack Pye, belting the referee over the head with a wash bowl! There were Morris Dancers skipping and displaying their skills, gymkhanas and mock battles with terrific bangs and clouds of smoke. Army and Navy teams would race each other dismantling guns and one year the Canadian Mounties came over. They thrilled everybody with their long, steel-tipped lances and superb horsemanship, as they performed intricate manoeuvres around the arena. My admiration of those red coated horsemen was total and I dreamed of joining them one day.

After 'bunking-in', my first objective was to get beneath the stand with its slatted seats and green canvass sides to search the grass for any coppers that may have fallen through. It was usually worthwhile but often risky as there were policemen stationed at either end of the stand. However, it wasn't too difficult to avoid their clutches as they were usually more interested in what was happening in the arena than a few scruffy individuals scurrying around beneath the stand. I once found a '10s note' and was so overcome with surprise at having 'trousered' such bounty, I couldn't contain myself.

"Look what I've found!" I shouted to my fellow scavengers. As I did so, the canvass was pulled back and a policeman's helmet appeared. I didn't hang around to see who was underneath it, but took to my heels and scarpered!

My favourite place was the fairground, but which young lad wouldn't be fascinated by the shouting and laughing of people on the rides and the animated urging of the stall-holder persuading revellers to part with their money. I loved the multi-coloured lights that were looped from stall to stall, and would watch as they swung gently to and fro in the breeze. I rarely saw so many and whenever I did, for some reason, they almost moved me to tears.

The Boxing Booth always attracted a large crowd and the shouting and cheering that came from the steamy tent was like a magnet to me and my mates. One year, Mr Symons, who lived off Rawson Road, and himself a handy fighter, decided to accept the challenge being offered and promptly flattened their champion and three others he was put against. We cheered and yelled and when he came outside he gave us a silver shilling each! It was revealed later that he was given a sum of money on the understanding that he wouldn't come near the tent for the rest of the week!

The side shows were full of nature's `misfits'. I can vividly recall seeing a two headed sheep, a five legged dog, the smallest woman on earth and awful jelly-looking objects in large bottles. I've no idea what was in those cloudy containers, and didn't want to find out. I suppose today I could receive `supportive counselling' to relieve my trauma!

Beyond the side shows were the penny arcades and major rides. The rides were usually beyond my pocket, although now and then I was able to sneak one by jumping on the side and grabbing the bars, rather like jumping a bus. One night the ride boss pushed me off and I went hurtling through the air. I came to grief at the feet of a policeman, who hauled me to my feet and threw me out of the showground.

"I'll lock you up next time I see you!" he shouted after me. Needless to say, I was back in again ten minutes later.

Generally though, I headed in the direction of the penny arcades. Penny after precious penny I slipped into those slots. Then, as though requiring a great amount of skill, I slowly released the lever that sent a steel ball whizzing around the track to fall between the pins that guarded holes marked "Win" or "Lose". My hands would grip the side of the machine tightly, my breath was held and wide expectant eyes followed the dancing ball as it tripped delicately along the top of the pins. Inevitably, the breath was expelled from my lungs like a pricked balloon and my body relaxed as the ball disappeared down the hole marked "Lose". I became convinced that the `Lose' hole had a magnet behind it!

As evening wore on the flattened grass became dark and slimy and after the tramping of hundreds of feet the earth became yielding and gluey. There were always eager youngsters waiting their turn in front of the flicker machine called "What The Butler Saw". After inserting a penny you looked through a large curved eye-piece and cranked a handle. It showed a lady preparing for bed, but much to our dismay she took so long getting ready that when the flicker ended she was still fully clothed! Cranking the handle quicker didn't help. Either the butler was disturbed at his task or he shut his eyes when a gentleman should!

The Roll-a-Penny stalls, although simplicity itself, were one of my favourites. The surface was divided into squares marked 1d, 2d, 3d and so on. Every so often, a square, I suspect slightly smaller than the rest, was marked at 2/-. At intervals around the stall elevated pieces of wood with a groove down the centre enabled you to roll your pennies in whichever direction you chose. The coin had to land in the square and no part of the line had to be touched. Even the merest hint was sufficient for your penny to be snatched away.

"On the line. Hard luck!" the stall-holder would say." Try again!" The losing coin would then disappear into a huge pocket in his apron. My pennies invariably rolled like buckled bicycle wheels and spun onto a line or skittered swiftly over the oilcloth surface to fall into a sort of "No Mans Land" gully at the back.

Even today I cannot resist rolling a few coins when I visit a fairground. I'm sad to say the result is still the same. Nowadays, of course, they don't hold galas. The cost of running them is too high and besides charities are run on more efficient and sophisticated lines. It's a shame for I always enjoyed them and I feel sure my childhood was richer for it. I was an 'Artful Dodger', it's true, but strange as it may seem I think it helped me to appreciate things and the feelings of others as I grew into manhood.

Lamps

Binmen

Above:
Crosby Road, Seaforth

Left: Dad

Opposite:
Seaforth Barracks

Seaforth Road looking east

Top of Seaforth Road, 1943

Chapter 11

I was lowering myself, with a bulging jumper, from a wall in South View near Waterloo Town Hall, when suddenly an authoritive voice boomed,

"Oi, you! Come here!"

It was a policeman. He was standing some distance away from me and had I decided to 'leg it' I could have left him standing, yet I walked submissively toward him. In those days, it was just something you did. He could have been a hundred yards away, it would have made no difference, I would still have surrendered meekly! Authority was to be respected and it usually was. When asked for your name and address by a policeman, you gave it to him. If, on the other hand, you gave him a false name and address he would say, 'come on, now. Your real one!' I could never understand how he knew I was lying! I was caught many times by the police for either 'sapping' or for being in places I shouldn't have and made to give my name and address. After a good belt on the ear, which generated heat for ages and stung all the way home, He promised that 'I will be calling to see your dad'. From that moment, I lived in fear!

Many a night I have sat at home waiting for a rat-a-tat on the door, my knees knocking in case it was the police. That would have guaranteed a hiding from my dad. As bad and painful as that would have been, it was at least swift and over with quickly. With my mam on the other hand it was a long, drawn out affair with slaps and pinches and worst of all, twisting the fleshy parts of your arm. She also had a habit of slapping you in the middle of sentences, and very often to the beat of whatever tune happened to be playing on the wireless at the time!

"How dare you . . ." (slap!), "bring the police . . ." (slap!), "to my door!" (slap!). "What will . . ." (slap!), "the neighbours . . ."(slap!), "think!" (slap!) Is it any wonder that I never liked Victor Sylvester?

About a week later, I was sitting on the warm tarmac in the middle of Sandringham Road with Jimmy, where we'd spent the last hour trying to prise 'cats-eyes' from their rubber seating. I threw down my knife in disgust when, after all the trouble I had gone to, I discovered they wern't 'ollies' after all. Instead, we were confronted by metal tubes with reflective glass in one end!

"Arr eh!" I snorted, "all that work for nothin'! I thought they were round, didn't you Jim?" Jimmy had thrown down his knife in disappointment, too, but had broken the handle in doing so. He looked horror stricken and was desperately pressing the two parts together in the forlorn hope they would fuse into one neat joint. Failing, he stared woefully at the broken handle.

"My mam will kill me when she sees this!" he wailed.

"Why, Jimmy?" I asked, concerned, "what's up?"

"This is what's up!" he moaned, indicating the broken knife. "This is the knife me mam uses to peel spuds".

"Maybe she won't miss it," I said optimistically.

"She's bound to!" Jimmy answered. "We've only got the one and we're having chips for tea tonight. She told my dad this morning. I've had it! I've had it now!" he repeated, shaking his head sadly. He looked totally dejected, but then I had an idea.

"Tell you what, if we take it to ours and glue it, she might not notice that its been broken." Jimmy's face relaxed for a second before clouding over once more.

"Its no use. She's bound to notice. I mean, look at it".

"Maybe she will, but it's worth a try," I retorted. "Better than a hiding, isn't it?" Images of thick ears and slaps on the head flickered before Jimmy's eyes and before you could say 'it wasn't my fault, mam', we were in our back kitchen pouring generous globs of rubber solution onto the broken parts of the knife.

"That's what they use for mending punctures in bike tubes, isn't it, Charlie?" There was concern in Jimmy's tone.

"Yeah", I said winking, "and those patches never come off, do they?" Jimmy smiled and winked back, but without the same conviction. He had, though, brightened considerably.

"There, how's that?" I asked, laying the knife on the table like a recovering patient. "You nip home and put it in the drawer to go hard. And grab a butty while you're there because I thought later we could go 'sappin'. What do you think?" Jimmy was all for it and it was fairly obvious that the more distance he could put between himself and his mam's knife drawer, the better.

I suppose there are many slang terms for nicking apples and pears. I've heard it called 'scrumpin' and 'crackin', but to us it was always known as 'sappin'. There were a few places we liked to call 'our regulars', but they were night-time visits and as it was mid-afternoon, it needed to be somewhere we had never been before, with plenty of cover. It was while we were racking our brains to think of somewhere that Ronnie and Arthur came running up.

"Hi, what are you doin' this 'avvy'?" Ronnie asked.

"Well, nothing special. We were thinking of going sappin but we can't think where. Somewhere new".

We sat on the pavement facing the warm sun, discussing likely places to go, but for one reason or another they were rejected. Then Arthur, or 'Arty' as we called him, sat bolt upright.

"I know a place!" he said excitedly, "Park House!".

"Where?" Jimmy asked.

"Park House," repeated Arty. "I saw it yesterday from the top of the bus. There's loads of apples, and pears, too . . . I think," he added doubtfully.

"Do you mean the nursing home by South Road?" I asked.

"Yeah, that's the place. Do you know it?"

"I should do, I walk past it nearly every Saturday after the pictures. I never knew there was an orchard there, though. Is it wide open or is there any cover where we can hide?"

"I dunno", he said. "There seemed to be a few bushes. I only saw it for a second because the driver 'stepped on the gas', but it looked a 'cinch'," enthused Arty, ending with a 'gangsterism' he had picked up from a Jimmy Cagney film. Arty always used gangster terms when he spoke, and even sounded like Humphrey Bogart. When he ran away he was 'keeping one step ahead of the G-men'. If we went to look at something we were 'casing the joint'! Cars were 'jallopies' and money was 'dough'!

He wasn't known for his speed of thought, which made him an easy target in school, but we always protected him. He was a kind and very likeable lad and his generosity could take your breath away. He was, though, the most accident-prone person I ever met in my life. I never knew anyone like him. If there was a hole anywhere in the Crosby area to fall down, Arty found it. If there was a raised kerb on the length of South Road, he would trip over it. Dogs travelled miles just to bite him. He was a walking disaster area and he could drive you mad with the things he did. But he was our mate and he was in our gang because we liked him.

Before going to 'Waterloo Park House', we crossed the road to watch the monkey running along the wall of the Liver Pub bowling green. I never knew what breed it was, but there was always a gathering when it was let outside, and passers-by fed it with nuts and little tit-bits. Most people who shopped in South Road liked to watch the antics of the monkey, except maybe one particular lady who fed it a tit-bit on the end of her umbrella. The monkey snatched the brolly from her and slung it under a passing bus!

"Ouch!" shouted Arty loudly as he dropped from the wall into Park House, and somehow managed to land in the only clump of nettles within twenty yards of him.

"Shush!" I said angrily, "someone will hear you".

"But it doesn't 'alf 'urt". he said, rubbing his legs furiously. "You wouldn't like it."

"And you'll like it even less if I throw you back in them," I said in a hoarse whisper. "So shut up!"

To our left a group of ducks took turns dipping their heads beneath the surface of the lake foraging for food and, apart from a noisy magpie, the coast was clear. We tucked our jumpers down our trousers in preparation to load up. Ronnie and Jimmy ran forward bent double and started climbing the nearest trees. I moved to the right to investigate what proved to be a heavily laden pear tree and Arty sprinted over to the left. In less than two minutes, I had filled my jumper and dropped out of the tree. Further over, Ronnie and Jimmy had done the same and we waited for Arty to come down. Suddenly, there was a shout.

"Oi! Stop right there!"   Which was precisely the kind of motivation we needed to take to our heels and 'leg it' to the wall where we could make good our escape. The shouting became louder and more demanding, then suddenly it was raised in triumph.

"Ah, ha!" he said, with obvious satisfaction. "Well, I've got one of you." We turned at the wall and looked back in time to see Arty dangling from the tree by his jacket. In his haste to escape, his coat had caught on a branch and he was stuck fast. The man was tugging at Arty, who then crashed to the ground, winded and in no condition to make a break for it. In an instant the man had him by the scruff of the neck and was shaking him. He turned to us and thrust Arty before him like a rag doll.

"You might as well give up, too, 'cos I'll get your names from him." And so saying, clipped Arty across the back of the head! It went completely against the grain to surrender, especially after getting clean away, but after a speedy consultation we agreed that we couldn't let Arty take the 'rap' alone. We turned ourselves in. Our delighted captor marched us ahead of him, muttering 'you thought you could get away with it, eh? You've got to get up early to kid me. Cheeky buggers!' Eventually, after walking through a maze of corridors and endless flights of stairs, we were ushered in front of a stern looking nun, seated behind a large desk, writing.

"I caught these lads stealing apples, Mother. And I thought you might want to deal with them." said the man, wringing his cap and looking at his feet. She continued writing for a few moments then sat back and looked at us for what seemed an eternity while we shuffled from one foot to the other!

"Did they do any damage to the trees, Joe ?" she asked in a soft voice that carried a trace of an irish accent.

"No, Mother. And in their defence they did give themselves up when I caught this one." He pushed Arty forward who managed to trip on the edge of the rug and sprawl across the Mother Superior's desk. Arty recovered with surprising speed and sprang back to join us.

She pushed her chair back and came around the desk to us. She was a small woman, but her huge butterfly hat and large, puffy habit, overwhelmed us. As she looked at each of us in turn, it seemed to me there was the faintest suggestion of a smile about her lips.

"Don't you boys know its wrong to steal?" she asked, but without waiting for a reply, continued. "It is wrong in the eyes of God, not to mention the law. Didn't they teach you that in school?" We nodded and mumbled, then she continued. "Since Joe assures me you caused no damage, I won't punish you or send for the police if . . ., if you promise me you will never try to steal apples from here again. Now, I want you all to say a 'Hail Mary' and ask our Blessed Lady for forgiveness".

We looked at our feet and shuffled again, then after mumbling our 'Hail Marys', she said,

"In future, if you want any apples, you must come and ask and I'll see what I can do. And now Joe, you can see them off the premises"

Once we were back in Haigh Road, we breathed a sigh of relief.

"I thought we were for it then," said Jimmy.

"So did I!" said Arty. After making his usual kind of comment about being glad the 'Feds' never turned up, his next remark had us laughing until we ached.

"I wasn't very 'appy about that Joe fella dragging us inside like tha'," he said, in all seriousness, "but his mam was good about it, wasn't she?"

Chapter 12

Feigning death, I slid slowly and deliberately to the ground, finally coming to rest crumpled against the wall. My would-be assassins crept closer to make sure I was dead. Their guns at the ready to 'finish me off' if I moved a muscle.

I watched through narrowed eyelids as the two bushwackers crept closer, then as the hazy figures moved to one side, I sprang up and grabbed 'Fingers' Thomson around the neck. With one hand on his gun I levelled it at 'Klondyke' Pete who instinctively fired at the same time.

'Paquew!', 'Paquew!'.

It sounded like one shot but both assailants knew it was the end and they crumpled in a twisted heap. After a moment or two they jumped to their feet.

"You cheated! I shot you first!" shouted Jimmy.

"No, you didn't, I was only wounded." I pointed to my shoulder. "You got me 'ere".

"I should've finished you off when I 'ad the chance," he said indignantly.

"Yeah? Well, you don't get Hopalong Cassidy that easy. I've been doggin' your trail for ages. I could've let you 'ave it anytime."

"No, you couldn't, 'cos Ron had you covered from the side . . ."

It was the same after every Saturday morning matinee. We would burst from the Winter Gardens in Waterloo itching to emulate our heroes and always ended up arguing. We had just settled it once and for all, in a strip of woodland in Walmer Road, the scene of many a battle. Only last week Crazy Horse and a band of Oglala Sioux attacked a wagon train there and it took an hour to chase them off! This week old scores had to be settled so we had a major shoot-out, and although the 'baddies' tried their usual dirty tricks, Hopalong Cassidy won because the 'goodies' always did!

William Tell was shown one morning and we dashed home to organise our gear. We tried blackmail, and threatened violence trying to persuade my younger sister Ann to stand against the wall with an apple on her head, but she wouldn't co-operate. We assured her that we were 'dead shots', but she insulted us by saying we were rubbish and couldn't hit the side of our shed! She did, though, allow us to chalk her outline on the wash-house door. Later, as I looked at the amount of arrows sticking from the head area of the chalked outline, I thought maybe she was right to refuse! The game came to an abrupt end when my final arrow shattered the window of the wash-house and pinned one of my mam's 'smalls' to the boiler top. Before my dad had opened the back door to investigate what all the noise was, we were off and running!

A week earlier when Robin Hood had been shown at the 'Wints', we all wanted to be Robin and as that wasn't possible, we settled the argument by seeing who could spit the furthest. I never came in the 'meg specs' when it came to spitting, so I was cast as Will Scarlet. Armed to the teeth with our best 'bow an' arrows' we set off for 'King Kongs Island' in Brook Vale.

The Sheriff's men went to the 'tennis court' end and we, the goodies, went to the pond end. The idea was to head towards the centre stalking each other and, if we could, destroy the Sheriff's camp! Many minutes went by without us spotting a soul, but then a movement caught my eye and there down in a hollow were some of the Sheriff's men. I put my fingers to my lips to 'shush' Mick and suggested to the others that we charge down into the hollow shouting and firing our bows as we ran. Camouflaged heads bobbed up and down in agreement and at a given signal we charged. Or at least, I did! My 'chums' had hotfooted the other way and as I bounded into their midst I was promptly captured! The stalking continued for another half an hour, but I wasn't able to take part, being tied to a tree at the time!

We once saw Flash Gordon take on the 'Clay People' in an

underground city that you could only get into through a mountain that split apart to allow spacecraft through. The Emperor Ming had Flash and his companions captured and transported to his kingdom, but Flash was able to fight off the Clay People and force them to retreat. It was brilliant, but the argument about who was going to play Flash Gordon continued when we came out! In the end we agreed to let 'Todger' be Flash. He had bushy blond hair and the biggest ears, but the real reason was he had the only serviceable steering cart available at the time and later we wanted to convert it into a spacecraft!

After lunch, Ronnie, Jimmy and myself headed to Todger's and together we formulated a plan. With the aid of a few pieces of plywood and some bent nails, which took longer to straighten out than do the job, we converted Todger's cart into a passable spacecraft. A brush-pole pushed through some lino' to form a cone at the front gave it a streamlined effect and a plywood cowl made it look solid. Steering was made possible by lying flat on the cart and looking through a slit situated low down in the cowl. We thought if wind resistance was minimised, it would go faster. We had discovered aerodynamics and didn't know it!

The front gate was our mountain. One of us crouched behind the hedge with a piece of string attached to the gate and at a given command pulled it open. When the craft passed safely through, we let it swing back. The cart would continue down the side passage and at the end do a sharp left turn onto the grass, then it was scootered back. It was a great success until Todger decided to improve matters.

"I've been thinking," said Todger, one of life's great thinkers, "if two of you push me from the top of Dewlands Road until I shout 'let go' and someone is at the gate to open it, I could get enough speed up to circle the garden and come out of the gate again in one sweep. Wouldn't that be 'brillo'?" We all agreed that it would, indeed, be brillo!

We pulled the cart to the top of the street and when Todger

was all set, Ronnie and I shoved the cart for all we were worth.

"Let go!" Todger shouted. It all went wonderfully well and the cart flew down the road and Todger could be seen correcting the steering when necessary. All Ronnie and I could see was his blond hair flicking about in the wind and his feet dangling over the back end of the spacecraft!

"Now!" he shouted, and Jimmy opened the gate to allow the spacecraft to enter Mountain City. We raced after him to see if he managed to circle the garden and come out again. What we found was total chaos! Todger's mam, who had decided to hang a 'few bits' on the line to air, was blind to Todger's approach. As his view was restricted to an oblong of a few square inches, the inevitable happened. We all shouted at the same time.

"Look out!"

Todger's mam took one look from behind the sheet and shrieked! She gallantly tried to take evasive action, but she was too slow, too late. The spacecraft picked her up as neatly as a carpet sweeper and she ended up straddling the cowl like a bronco rider. Ronnie and I appreciated the finer qualities of this because we hadn't long seen "Bronco Billy And The Panhandle Rustlers" and there was a marked similarity in the way . . . well, you know what I mean! The cart, which was probably doing about 20 mph, came to a sudden halt as it hit the edge of the path and Todger's mam shot from the spacecraft's cowl like a launched missile and sailed, most unladylike, over a bed of 'Webbs Wonderful Lettuce', coming to rest in Todger's dad's prize chrysanthemums.

If more evidence were needed of my lack of moral fibre, once again I provided it. While Todger's shouts for help where whipped away in the afternoon breeze, Ronnie, Jimmy and me were legging it up the 'jigger' behind Ionic Street, heading for home!

More often than not, it was bedlam during the matinee shows. Apart from the cheering and booing, there would be fighting, shouting, missiles being thrown about and very often

an assertive voice yelling, " an' I'll see you outside after!"
Somehow, though, we never missed a single word that was
'yelled' from the screen. At the Odeon, before any films were
shown, we would have singing and an organ would magically
appear from beneath the stage, complete with organist, playing
a variety of tunes. Words appeared on the screen and a bounc-
ing ball frolicked across the top in time to the music. At some
stage a spotlight swept the auditorium and whoever it stopped
on received a free ice-cream. I wanted that spotlight to stop on
me more than anything in the world, but in all the years I was
going, it never even came close.

The Queen's down South Road and the 'Wints' were great
cinemas, too, and evoke special memories. I mourn their
passing. I don't envy the children of today with their computer
games and hand held 'gameboys'. They will never experience
Saturday matinees as I did. They will never understand what it
was like to gallop home, slapping your backside, with the top
button of your coat fastened around your neck, the remainder
flapping in the wind as you pushed your mount to greater
effort. I watch children now with their replica football kits and
Batman outfits and see how much they take these things for
granted. They do not enjoy the raw, imaginative fun that we
did. I shake my head in disbelief when I see the computer games
and electrical toys that they have now. My grandchildren
receive more on one Christmas morning than I did in all my
young years, but I don't envy them. I can put my hand on my
heart and say, looking back all those years ago, that I wouldn't
trade my childhood with anyone.

Chapter 13

Once, during one of the Odeon matinees, it was announced that due to a paper shortage in the country, there was to be a scrap paper drive organised, and the group who collected the most would win a prize of five `bob' and an ice cream! To me and my mates, it represented a small fortune and, although we knew it was going to be hard work and would take up most of our spare time, we went all out to win it!

After school hours and at weekend's, we were usually seen out and about knocking on doors trying to persuade the occupants to hand over their old newspapers. However, progress was slow and it became obvious we had to increase our work rate. The need to improve our tonnage was hammered home when we happened to bump into one of the opposing teams with a cart loaded so high it needed someone to walk in front of them waving a red flag!

In order to catch up, Jimmy and me took the decision to `sag' school the following day. We added a considerable amount to our `stash', but the danger of being spotted by the cycling School Inspector, or our mam's, was too great, so we only did it the once.

The horse drawn salvage carts that plodded around the district were, as we saw it, in direct opposition and seemed to be achieving a considerable amount of success. It was, therefore, agreed that we would share in their success by `nicking' what we could from them! The sliding shutters on the cart were extremely heavy and it required a plan to extract as much paper as possible with the minimum of fuss. The plan drawn up was simple, but effective. When the men went around to the back of a particular address, we pulled our cart alongside. Two of us stood on top and shoved the lid open, while the third grabbed what he could before they returned. We were very successful and our stockpile rapidly trebled in size until the day, on hearing the men coming back, we panicked and the sleeve of my jersey became trapped in the shutter as it was lowered. Jimmy and Ronnie scarpered, but I was left with little choice but to stay where I was and face the consequences. I had steeled myself for a right hiding, but when the two men came back, they just started laughing and left me where I was.

"Get on, Sally," one of them said, clicking his tongue, "make your way home, lass."

Sally, who knew the drill well enough, pricked up her ears and even quickened her step, no doubt thinking about chomping on mouthfuls of succulent hay and curling up in a warm stable for the night. I had to walk alongside the salvage cart on my tippy toes all the way to the corporation yard, my arm held in a permanent salute before I was eventually released! The corporation workers howled with laughter when we entered the yard, and I could feel my face burning with indignation. I tried very hard to walk away with as much dignity as I could muster, but as soon as I was out of sight I took to my heels and fled!

It became necessary at one stage to update my steering cart to accommodate the piles of paper I was hoping to get, and so I added sides to it, hinged for quick removal for when we resumed our racing! In effect, I altered it from the basic model, to the GTI 'Ghia' with carpeted seat! We needed to double our efforts in the paper drive as the last day for collecting was looming closer, and it was agreed that to stand any chance we would need to pull out all the stops.

On the morning of the final day we were feeling rather dejected as we observed our meagre pile of paper and were about to call it a day. It was a dull day and moral had dipped to an all time low. Even one or two spots of rain spattered the pavement.

"I'll tell you what," I said, trying to sound more enthusiastic than I really was, "let's give it one more shot. Let's try down Victoria Road then back up Gt. Georges Road. If we don't get anythin', we'll 'ead home. What d'ya say?"

Ronnie and Jimmy nodded in agreement and we headed off. We were nearing the bottom of `Vicky' Road with little to show for it, when a voice behind us shouted.

"Hey, you lads".

We turned to see a man beckoning to us.

"Are you collecting paper? I've got some in my garage if you want it." He looked at our carts and smiled, "you'll need more than those to carry it, though!"

He led us to his garage and what we saw took our breath away. Piled from floor to ceiling were bundles of magazines, which turned out to be medical journals. There must have been thousands of them! He was right though, our carts wouldn't be adequate enough, so we took them home and returned with upgraded, fully sprung deluxe models, our prams! We were not to be denied.

It took all morning and well into the afternoon before we finally emptied his garage and transported it all to the Odeon. He even gave us a shilling each for, as he put it, `getting shut of it'. Surely, that five `bob' was ours? Unfortunately, it wasn't! The following Saturday the winners were announced from the stage, and we came second to a troop of scouts. It would be foolish to say we wern't disappointed, because we were, but we weren't too dejected. After all, there was only three of us compared to a whole `posse' of scouts, and we did get `half a dollar' and an orange lolly for second prize!

We even went to the Mayor's house to have tea and be thanked by him personally. My dog Mick was more than pleased that the scrap drive was over because now it meant we could concentrate on the important things in life, like checking the marsh in Brook Vale to see if the pair of mallards we saw a few days ago, had nested.

Our steering carts were very important to us and care was lavished on them to keep them in peak condition. Very often we would experiment with new ideas in order to gain the upper hand over the other competitors. When Arty turned up one day with springs fitted onto the axles of his cart, it caused great interest.

"I'll show you guys how to race a cart." he said, a smug expresssion on his face.

We gathered around to see his first test run and watched as he approached the kerb. There was a twanging noise and Arty, holding onto the steering rope for dear life, continued down Hereford Road as if he were mounted on a giant pogo stick. It was back to the drawing board for Arty! We often held street races in our carts, but although they were for fun, there were two prestige titles to compete for. The Brook Vale Bridge title, and the Cambridge/Sandringham Road circuit title. Both honours were competed for at regular intervals so, although you might have won the championship the week previous, everything could change at the next `meet' and your crown could be snatched from your head.

The road circuit title was a simply a case of who could complete two laps, each of a quarter mile, the fastest. Even though I was small of stature, I was a natural steering cart racer. My cart was in tip-top condition and always well greased. It also had chrome wheel rims which I kept highly polished and had a devastating effect on the opposition! If ever I had my nose in front, it was a hefty pyscological blow when the sun glinted from my wheels, and I began to widen the gap. From that moment it was a question of who was going to finish second!

The `Bridge' title was probably the easiest of the two to compete in, but required a little more nerve and a lot more luck. The idea was to gain as much speed as possible down the slope and once a certain point had been reached, which was carefully monitored by stewards, you stopped `scooting' your-self and free-wheeled as far as possible. As it was in the days when the bridge gave access for two-way traffic, competitors nerves were stretched to the limit as they weaved their way in and out of on-coming vehicles, especially coaches returning from Brook Vale playing field. It wasn't unknown for some

71

competitors nerves to crack under the strain and at the last minute veer off course down the embankment, ending up in the allotments!

We did contemplate starting a new race called `Bomb Ally'. The idea was to run a gauntlet behind the bombed houses in Cambridge Road while everyone chucked stones at you. If you completed the run unscathed you became champ. Unfortunately, it never got off the ground. We had persuaded Arty to try a dummy run but he ended up with a split head and cut knees and so we had to abandon the idea!

Brook Vale bridge is on a one-way traffic system these days, but I always approach it warily in case some idiot in a steering cart is coming the other way!

Chapter 14

I looked back to see if she was still following and saw her darting into the 'jigger' at the back of Chestnut Avenue.

"Go away!" I shouted, "we don't want you with us! We don't want girls in our gang!" Alice reluctantly emerged from the jigger, shouting defiantly,

"Why not? I'm as good a climber as any of you and I'm better at throwin' as well." For added emphasis she picked up a stone and flung it at us. It caught Harry Symes on the foot, but before he could retaliate, Alice was up and running!

"I don't want to be in your stupid gang, anyway!" she yelled over her shoulder, "you're all ugly and I hate you!"

I shuddered when I thought of what it must be like to be a girl. It's a well known fact that they can't do the things boys do. They like to think they can, but . . . well, only a few days earlier Sarah Bench fastened onto us and try as we might to shake her off, we couldn't, so in the end we relented and allowed her to stay. And what happened? As soon as Jimmy put a frog down her neck, she started crying and ran home to tell her mam! We do it to each other all the time and we don't give it a second thought. If you just squirm around for a bit, it drops out of the end of your shorts and, anyway, she wouldn't put one in her mouth so how could she even think of being in our gang! They were just not as good as us at climbing, fighting, catching fish or exploring. How can you play Cowboys or Cops and Robbers with a girl?

Girls are soppy. They like to play with dolls and prams and draw Hop-Scotch on the pavement and play house. They skip to silly songs like 'In The Meadow, Stands A Lady' and 'All In Together' There's one thing they are pretty good at, although I wouldn't have admitted it to the rest of the lads; they tuck their skirt into their knickers and play 'Two Balls' against the wall.

I've never tried it, of course. But it looks easy enough and if a soppy girl can do it, so could I!

On one occasion, I really got into trouble. Becky Thurber and her mate Linda Sinnot followed us to an old empty house in Adelaide Road, Seaforth. They didn't think we knew, but they'd been spotted skulking near the old American Motor Depot, so we laid on a little surprise for them. As they came sneaking in the door, we grabbed them and threw them in the cellar and wedged the door tight with an old beam! They didn't half carry on, shouting and yelling. Then they started to cry.

"Let's out! It's dark down here! And there's mice!"

"Shut up!" shouted Jimmy   "you'll be alright. We'll let you out in a minute." Putting his finger to his lips he motioned for us to sneak away.

"We won't follow you anymore, honest," shouted Becky, but we couldn't hear their shouting and pleading because we were racing to the canal for a swim. The 'Broken Bridge' was the best place to swim because it had a sandy bottom and you were less likely to stand in anything nasty. A few weeks earlier I had been swimming along, head down, trying to learn the 'Australian Crawl' when I bumped headlong into a dead dog! Another common occurrence was to suddenly find yourself swimming among some nameless scrapings discharged into the canal by the many tanneries built along its banks!

Making its way slowly toward our swimming area was a fully loaded barge, being pulled along the tow-path by a weary looking horse. The bargee at the tiller looked hot and grimy and was no doubt looking forward to a rest and something to eat further up the canal. We all jumped out while he skilfully manouvered his barge through the narrows, then, once he had passed, we dived back in again.

It was late in the afternoon and as the sun was beginning to descend rapidly below the horizon, we decided to call it a day. It wasn't until we were almost home that Jimmy and me were suddenly hit with the same thought.

"Bloody hell, the girls!"

For us, enjoying ourselves swimming in the canal, the afternoon had flown by, but I had a sickening feeling in the pit of my stomach when I realised they had been locked in the cellar for almost four hours! When we eventually reached the door leading to the cellar, the first thing that struck me was that it was deathly quiet and I became a little uneasy! I'd had visions of them clamped in each others arms kicking out at packs of girl-eating mice, but it was so quiet my first thought was that the mice had succeeded in devouring them! I felt the first pangs of guilt at forgetting about them and pulled the beam away from the door. Immediately the girls burst out, frightened and crying. They started swinging punches at us and a few of them hurt, too! Their tear stained faces were twisted in anger and hate and they were sobbing and kicking out at us.

"Just you two wait!" Linda Sinnot shouted. "I'm going to tell me mam when I get home and she will go to see yours and I wouldn't like to be you!"

"And, I'm going to tell our Terry," Becky joined in "he's bigger than the two of you put together, and he'll batter you!" After aiming a kick at me, which thankfully missed, they ran off hand in hand. She was right about one thing, though, their Terry was definitely capable of battering us both at the same time! I looked at Jimmy and knew he felt as uneasy as I did. In the weeks to follow, it required a certain amount of skill to keep as much distance as possible between Terry and myself. However, I wasn't able to avoid my mam! When Linda's mam told her what I had done, my feet never touched the ground! I was playing football in the street, practising my Stanley Matthews body swerves, when she shouted for me to 'get in here!' I could tell by the tone of her voice that I was in for it and I wasn't wrong! It was a few hours before the exposed parts of my body stopped stinging and a full week before I was allowed out to play.

Vicky, who lived next door to me in Ewart Road, Seaforth,

was a slight exception to the general rule. She didn't try to tag along if we went off collecting shrapnel or exploring newly bombed houses, she was quite content to sit and play with her doll until we returned. If I sustained a cut or a knock she showed concern and was always ready to blow on it or cluck sympathetically. She had a crush on me and I think she was my first girlfriend. Whenever Vicky saw me outside, either playing 'ollies' or kicking a football, she would try to join in the fun. Once, not long after Christmas she came running out to join me where I was sitting on the edge of the pavement.

"What did Father Christmas bring you, Charles?" she asked, toying with the ribbons in her hair.

"Lots of games an' a train set," I lied, "but I'll be gettin' new 'footy' boots as well, when he gets a chance to bring them!"

Vicky's brow had furrowed slightly as she continued to fiddle with her ribbons.

"But why didn't he bring them for you last week and save himself a journey?"

"He must have had too much to carry, because he left a note telling me he'd get them as soon as he can. Me mam said he does that sometimes."

"I got Millie" she said, pushing a rag doll with a patchwork frock toward me. "Isn't she lovely?"

"Well, she's alright, I suppose," I said grudgingly, "but not as good as footy boots!"

I jumped to my feet and continued to kick my ball against the double doors opposite. Vicky cuddled Millie close and hummed her a lullaby, as she rocked her in her arms. It didn't look as though my other mates were coming out just yet, so I threw the ball into the vestibule and grabbed Vicky by the hand.

"C'mon," I said excitedly, Lets go to the park, the swings might be unlocked now."

That evening the siren rose and fell like a wailing Banshee. Everyone in the house was rushing around grabbing what they had been told to take when 'he came over'. My mam handed me a pillow. "Here son, you carry that for me, there's a good boy."

In a minute or two we were running with the rest of the crowd and soon we were safe in the cellar of Thompson Road School, except for my dad who was on fire watch outside! It was the noise that made him look up, he told us later, like the flapping of a tents fly sheet. The black parachute mine floated menacingly close to the school steeple before finally coming to rest at the rear of our house. The school shook and trembled for a long time after the explosion but thankfully remained intact! When the All Clear sounded, people emerged pale and bleary-eyed from wherever they had taken refuge from the bombing. They picked their way through the rubble strewn streets offering silent prayers that they still had a place they could call home. Our house had been reduced to a heap of rubble! Perched crookedly on top of the smoking pile was the cooker, which still contained the Sunday joint, now well and truly over-cooked! The soldiers, digging frantically in the smoking heap, breathed a sigh of relief when my dad told them we were all safe. They packed their gear together and piled into the back of a truck, presumably to dig for more victim's of the bombing.

Vicky and her mam hadn't gone to the shelter. They never used to bother. 'If it's got your name on it, it'll get you anyway' she used to say to my mam. Instead, they had taken refuge under the stairs. Vicky wouldn't be coming to play anymore. I wouldn't be taking her to the swing-park again. She wouldn't be sitting on the pavement with Millie, laughing when I miss-kicked the ball and fell over, and she never did see my new footy boots when I got them.

Chapter 15

The lead duck swung right and like a bullet headed in my direction, altering course slightly as it came across my line. I threw the Greener 12 bore shotgun to my shoulder, took a quick bead and fired. The kick of the load pushed me a little and I saw the duck stall as the charge of shot hit home. It folded its wings and dropped to earth about thirty yards away. Mick took off as soon as he heard the report and with uncanny instinct, pinpointed and retrieved the fallen bird. Light was increasing from the East but the frost had intensified as the night wore on. It was bitterly cold and we had been out all night. After catching the last train to Southport we had made our way back along the coast to Waterloo, our starting point.

With the necessary gear stowed into our packs we had arrived at Southport and were making our way in the direction of the marshes. No sooner had we left the sanctuary of the station when the first snow flakes began to fall and settle ominously on the pavement. It looked like it was going to stick and with no prospects of shelter for the night, there was no alternative but to proceed with the original plan. There were no trains going back until morning, so our bridges were well and truly alight!

"What d'you think, Charl?" asked Bill, an obvious reference to the weather.

"I don't think we have a choice now, Bill. Let's hope the weather improves a bit, eh? It took all day to persuade me mam to let me do this, so we'll have to make the best of it!"

"I didn't expect the snow, though." retorted Bill angrily, "of all the luck!"

Once on the marsh and away from the comparative shelter of the streets the wind seemed to increase in strength, the sleet stinging our exposed faces. In the distance, grotesque shapes in the deserted amusement park stood out in sharp relief against the lights of the town, and somewhere to our left a frustrated motorist sounded his horn, in stark contrast to the silence of the marsh. The snow continued to fall, becoming heavier by the minute and whipped into my eyes causing me to walk with my head down and to one side. Suddenly, I slipped and sprawled face down into liquid mud! As I stood up, I slipped again and this time, fell backwards!

"Oh, no!" I yelled in anguish, "I don't believe it! I'll never get this cleaned off!"

"It's alright Charl," Bill shouted in triumph, "I've found your gun!"

"Sod you and the gun, look at the cut of me. Its a good job me mam can't see me now. I'd get a right hidin'."

After much cursing and searching we found a reasonably sheltered channel and settled in its lee from the unrelenting wind, waiting for the curlew to come and feed. The mud, with which I was liberally coated, had frozen as hard as clay and as I hugged the bank of the gully, I felt like something discarded from a potters wheel, and thoroughly miserable.

After what seemed an age we heard the unmistakable "coolie" of the curlew. Loading our guns we strained our eyes into the blackness, made worse by the falling sleet, for a glimpse of our quarry. We knew to ignore the first few, remaining out of sight as they flew over our position again and again. When at last they were satisfied it was safe, they turned and flew back to the main flock. A few minutes later the first flights came over. Whether it was the cold or just bad shooting I don't know, but we never bagged one. It was now two in the morning and we decided to make our way further along the coast.

For three or four miles we trudged through mud and shallow water, then in a deep trough we took shelter for a while to drink hot tea from the flask. Mick lay alongside me and seemed oblivious to the cold or the coating of snow on his back, but even so he appreciated a hot drink from my cup. While we were having a break it stopped snowing, giving us fresh heart, but almost immediately I could feel the frost in the air.

Although the snow had been bothersome it did help to keep the temperature bearable. Now, with frosty conditions plus the chill factor, my teeth began to chatter and I noted with grim irony, that I could chatter rhythmically! Where I had been soaked earlier plus perspiration from walking, my clothes became solid and unyielding. I had never been so cold, but then I'd never walked along the coast, in the middle of the night, during a blizzard. Bill was just as miserable and with the flask now empty our moral, like the cold, dropped another couple of degrees.

It was some time before I associated the distant chattering I could hear as being geese and not my teeth! With the tide having turned, they were coming off the fields to feed on the exposed mud flats. Peering from our sheltered hide we could just distinguish their shapes against the clear starry sky and they seemed lower than I'd seen them before. Maybe, with any luck, they would be within range of our 12 bores.

"Don't make a move, Bill. We might just bag a couple of these."

Bill didn't seem very enthusiastic and merely nodded, but I knew deep down he was as keen as mustard! We waited until they were directly above us before we moved and then, nothing. I couldn't move the trigger or the action lever! The entire mechanism had frozen solid. It was so frustrating and we both swore loudly to the heavens. It was as if the geese knew, because they flew even lower, mocking us with their cackling calls. I hugged the gun to my body and kept it there until the mechanism freed itself, by which time of course the geese were a long way off! Their cackling seemed louder as they headed further and further away as though sharing some hilarious joke, which perhaps they were. Grudgingly, we sloshed our way further up the coast, spurred on by the thought that every step took us nearer to a warm bed.

Occasionally, seagulls glided past, ghostly and silent. Do seagulls ever sleep, I wondered? A short distance away the tall sandhills seemed cold and uninviting. The wind plucked the loose sand from the high ridges and sent it spiralling upward, changing the shape of the hills forever. What would they look like in fifty or a hundred years from now, I thought. Would they still be there for people to admire or would the elements reduce them to insignificant little mounds? Traces of smoke spiralled upwards from the nearest hills, a sure sign that Jack the hermit was up and already preparing breakfast. It was a welcome sight. I wasn't sure if we had passed Jack's in the darkness and was delighted when I saw the smoke. There was always a welcome at Jack's and we often called in to chat when we came to explore the hills or the woods beyond. I nodded in the direction of the smoke.

"Let's call over to Jack's an' see if we can get a warm, eh Bill?"

"I'm all for tha'" answered Bill. "I could just go a cup of tea!"

Jack's home was part hut, part shored up dug-out, with a pot-bellied stove at one end. Even at that early hour, Jack greeted us with a friendly, though sleepy smile, and a few minutes later the kettle bubbled and hissed on top of the stove. With my hands clasped around a hot cup of tea I took the opportunity to look around Jacks home. There was a bed on one side, and a cupboard containing food and other personal items, took up the whole of the other side. Near to the entrance he had built a porch out of driftwood, which, as Jack said, 'helped to keep out that bloody nor' wester!' It was, though, very cosy and so it was with a certain amount of reluctance that we decided to press on and after thanking Jack for his hospitality, we left. I think, with very little effort, Mick could have been persuaded to stay and claw marks scored on either side of the door frame as I pushed him out, seemed to confirm this! However, once he realised that I really was on my way, he trotted by my side.   We arrived at Hall Road, and the erosion, around 6 o'clock in the morning and settled in behind some rocks to wait for the early morning flights of duck. I studied a small crab which seemed bent on climbing onto my wader. After a few abortive attempts, he tired of the game and scuttled beneath a rock with a final squirt of bubbles in my general direction.

In the event we didn't have too long to wait. There was a faint glimmer of light breaking from the East and through it we saw what looked like smoke haze, but was in fact hundreds of ducks. It took a couple of minutes for the first ones to reach our position then they streaked above us before we realised it. They seemed to come from every direction. I fired at the lead duck of a group to my left and watched where it hit the ground, then swung to my right as they were veering away. Again I hit the target and noted where it fell.

By now of course the whole flight were aware of our presence and had altered course, but we could see more heading our way and in the brief period of time before they reached us, we had retrieved our birds. I was luckier than Bill who only bagged one. We watched the approaching ducks with mounting scepticism thinking that the earlier skirmish would deter them from their line of flight, but it hadn't and soon my gun was up and punching my shoulder. After the flights had passed and the air was stilled of excited duck calls, we located our birds and were pleased to discover we had bagged six each.

During those hectic few minutes the light had improved and as the tide had not yet turned, many species of wading birds could be seen hopping and twittering across the cold, fog covered sandbanks. Flocks of dunlin flittered over the sand like ballerinas and oyster catchers could be seen goose-stepping in shallow pools. Dark shadowy outlines of ships breathing black smoke, buffeted their way up the river, seeking sanctuary in the shelter of the docks. Soon other people appeared on the beach. Hardy folk who, irrespective of the weather conditions, walked dogs or just strolled along enjoying the early morning air. Despite having risen early themselves, they looked at us with barely concealed awe as we trudged wearily along. With the arrival of daylight and having at least bagged some birds, we were in a happier frame of mind as we continued in the direction of Crosby.

As we trudged along the tide-line I looked at Bill and saw what was no doubt, a mirror image of myself, with one exception, I had a liberal coating of mud from head to toe! One thing was certain, I would have to sneak in the house. I couldn't let my mam see me like this or I'd never be able to do it again. Then again, I don't think I wanted to and I said as much to Bill!

"I don't think I'll be doing that again, Bill!"

"I'm bloody sure I won't!" he said vehemently. "In fact, I don't think I want to see this beach again for quite some time!"

"You're probably right," I answered. "I know we got a few ducks, but I think next time, . . .if there is a next time" I added hastily, "We'll head to Wales. It's good there."

Before very long the houses that earlier had been an indistinct grey ribbon on the horizon, took on a more solid, imposing shape and street lamps winked out as the clock reached it's allotted time span. Milkmen wrestled crates from their vans and tinkled their way up garden paths, in some cases eagerly awaited by a gown clad householder on the doorstep. Paper boys warily rode their bikes on the slippery pavement in a brave attempt to deliver their charges.

Thankfully, we boarded a bus that would take us the last few miles home. Tired, dirty and cold, we allowed its warm interior to envelope us. I am sorry to say that my ducks were not received with much enthusiasm. One or two members of the family made no attempt to hide their disgust, if not at the sight of the ducks, certainly at my appearance. I plucked and cleaned the ducks and left them by the oven as a gentle hint to my mam, then went to bed where I remained in a zombie-like state for ten hours!. When I eventually tottered downstairs it was evident, judging by the pitiful remains left in the pantry, that any disgust shown earlier had been shelved and that the smell of roasting fowl had proved irresistible! Mine was left for me on a large plate. Cold, over cooked and looking so very, very pitiful.

Chapter 16

The seagulls settled down facing the wind, their heads tucked into their breasts, large yellow beaks opening and closing noiselessly. Occasionally, one or two would cry in alarm and rise protesting into the swirling snow, annoyed at having to spread their wings to the cold, icy wind. A little further over a group of crows fought bitterly over some tit-bit that had tumbled from one of the bin wagons. I looked at the bleak landscape, at the reeds in the brooks bravely trying to resist the fierce wind, and I wondered at natures bounty in providing birds and animals with such warm protection against winter's icy blanket.

I huddled deeper into the hole I was digging and tied the string tighter around my waist. The bag at my side needed to be filled before I could call it a day, but when I looked inside my heart sank. There were barely enough cinders to start a fire, never mind last all night. It had been slow work this morning as the frost had been severe the night before, making it difficult to break through the frozen clinker-crust to reveal the still-warm cinders beneath. Occasionally, a piece of scrap copper or brass would come to light, which was slipped into a separate bag to 'weigh in' at a later date.

I tried to rub some circulation back into my hands but because of scratches caused by the sharp cinders, they were too sore, so I pushed them deep inside my pockets and huddled even further into the warm recesses of the hole I had dug. The wind had eased a little, and although it was still snowing, it was now possible to see much further than at any time since I'd arrived! I wasn't alone at my task. Here and there a bent back dotted the sky-line, each with but a single thought, to salvage as much coal as they could before it became too dark to see.

Our house always seemed to be cold and although this may well have been due to the general shortage of fuel in the country, a contributing factor was because there wasn't enough money coming into the home and buying coal was considered a luxury rather than a necessity.

My dad, though, was neither out of work, or lazy. His job simply didn't pay enough to cover our needs, so it was left to members of the family to assist where and how they could. Somehow, I ended up as 'procurement officer' for fuel, which put simply, meant I stole coal, coke or anything that would burn, from anywhere I could get it.

One of my more successful adventures was to push an old pram along Crosby Road to a point opposite the Odeon Cinema, where behind a high wall was a heap of shiny black coal. A couple of boards were missing from the dilapidated old gate and I was able to pass the coal out bit by bit until the pram was full. During the weeks that followed I made many trips 'behind the wall' and to my delight, it was constantly being added to. I couldn't get over my luck until one day I was chased the length of Crosby Road by an old man in a brown boiler suit. It was near Hougomont Avenue before he finally gave up and I was able to take a breather. Many months later I learned the mountain of black gold that I had visited - almost as a matter of right - was the fuel needed to fire the cinema's boilers. However, I must confess that had I known, it would not have made the slightest difference.

Another source of supply was behind Waterloo Grammar School. This, though, was always a night mission as it required scaling walls and picking my way across a number of rear gardens and to very carefully manoeuvre my way past a well lighted bus stop. That was the easy part. Taking a full bag back along those same walls, before dropping exhausted into my own back garden, was a little more difficult. My knees usually suffered badly during these raids. I can't recall a time when I didn't have plasters stuck all over them! One night I must have been spotted making my way around to the back, for as I crouched in the heap filling my sack, the school yard became flooded with light from the headlamps of two police cars. Abandoning my precious sack, I fled.

"We know you're there!" the policeman shouted "give yourself up!" Their calls growing fainter as I 'legged' it! I barely escaped the consequences of their clutches. To have been apprehended would have been disastrous, for then the 'game' would have been up.

There was a period of plenty at the Gas Works in Litherland Road, and if you had the means of carrying it away, they would fill it with coke for half-a-crown. My eldest sister Charlotte and I decided to take advantage of this offer, but we needed to borrow some method of transportation. A very kind neighbour of ours, Mr Roper, a foreman in the Corporation yard, agreed to lend us one of their handcarts. It was the later type with the large iron wheels that towered above me, but we were delighted and Charlotte and I pushed it to Litherland Road and back. A certain amount of skill was called for when we tried to circumnavigate the roundabout at the North Park, but we managed it and once we were on Linacre Road, heading toward the Lift Bridge, we were home and dry. Our prize was a heap of precious coke!

I did have other places I used to visit from time to time, but they were slim pickings and as such soon became exhausted. Often, I would push my cherished, but failing, pram to the shoreline to collect wood that had drifted in on the tide. Filling the pram was relatively easy, but pushing, and more often pulling it, through the soft, sugary consistency of the sand-hills made the going even tougher, but they had to be negotiated before I reached firm ground behind Potter's Barn. My nose dripped with exertion and I didn't have a clear space left on either arm of my jumper to wipe it on.

Once, having filled my pram with wood I was dragging it to firmer ground when it became stuck fast in the mud. It soon settled in over the axle and although I did everything in my power to pull it out, it was no use. The tide was coming in fast and I had to abandon it. Eventually, all that remained visible were the curved pram handles, a visual reminder of nature's cruelty. I was determined to retrieve my pram come what may and waited for the tide to turn. In those frugal days old prams didn't 'grow on trees', although quite how I was going to rescue it from the sucking mud, I didn't know.

I sat watching the ships on the river, throwing stones impatiently at the, now, ebbing tide. Suddenly the pram popped to the surface like a cork from a bottle. Unfortunately, my joy was short lived as it began to drift from me. Bobbing about, it reminded me of the Viking funeral in the film 'Beau Geste', only this time it was not bearing the remains of a gallant warrior, but my fire-wood! Did my pram become doomed to ride the oceans of the world forever like the 'Flying Dutchman' or did it just sail on and on and eventually settle as an unmarked wreck on some ocean bed? I never found out!

To be awakened early on a winters morning to go and queue outside a chandlers in order to buy 'Coal Bricks' was not something I relished, although I often had to do it. As the name suggests, a coal brick was a brick sized lump of coal dust, compressed to give it body. They gave out very little heat to speak of, but when you had nothing to burn, anything would do. Shops placed notices in their windows if they'd received a delivery. "Coal Bricks will be on sale at 8 a.m.", and for no reason I can think of, it was often a Sunday.

Very often there were none to be had anywhere, but a chandlers half-way down St Johns Road always managed to have some in stock. It was to that shop I was usually sent, still not quite awake, with a half-eaten round of fried bread sprinkled with sugar in my hand, to join others in an ever lengthening queue, with instructions to buy six or possibly eight. Sometimes the shopkeeper came to the door puffing out his chest with self importance, as he observed the queue.

"Only four bricks per person, I'm afraid." he would announce apologetically.

The queue of disgruntled shoppers shuffled their feet resignedly and resumed their conversations, which usually revolved around `what to get for the tea' or, more importantly, when the rationing was going to end! I settled down to wait for the door to open. I suppose it's to be remembered that there was a tremendous fuel shortage and selling was controlled. However, the disappointment was minor, for to have purchased any at all was an achievement.

When all else failed, it was a trip to the local tip where I discovered factories dumped 'clinker' from their boilers mixed with partly burnt coke. It meant hours of digging and sifting in the conditions I referred to at the beginning, but the end result was usually a fire that lasted all night. Having filled a sackful I would hurry home and sit by the fire painstakingly stacking the little pieces of cinder in the grate, until the whole hearth glowed red. Unfortunately, in my haste to fill the bag, tiny pieces of clinker would sometimes get mixed in. Occasionally, as we sat gathered around the fire, there would be a loud bang and the room would be sprayed with flying shrapnel, often with painful results. I wilted under the disapproving glare of my parents.

"Be a bit more careful of what you put in that bag, Charlie." said my dad, as another piece of 'clinker' ricocheted off the sideboard. "You'll have someone's eye out." Even so, I was never restrained or told not to go again!

But later came the reward for the cold and cut fingers endured that day. Sitting making toast from the glowing coals, my face and arms burning and mottled with the heat. I remember with affection, and a little pride, those 'Ovaltiney' days.

Chapter 17

On 20th November 1946, about the time my pram was bobbing erratically past the Bar Lightship, the 'S.S. Stormont' came to grief in Liverpool Bay carrying a cargo of livestock. It was one of those wild days when the sea boiled and heaved angrily, sending waves crashing onto the rocks and filled the air with flying spray. At the point where the sky meets the sea, it was a dark and seething place as wave after white capped wave rolled in to smash all in its path. It was doubtful that any animal could survive in such a rough sea, and none did. It wasn't long before the beach at Seaforth became littered with carcasses, and of course, news of what happened spread like wild-fire.

I was walking back from the 'chippie' with my mams lightly battered fish, when two of my mates, Ronnie and Jimmy, came running up to me, breathless and obviously very excited.

"Charlie! Guess what? There's been a shipwreck and loads of dead cows have been washed up on the beach! Some might still be alive! We're going down to have a look, are you coming?"

"Too right I'm coming," I replied. "Come with us while I take this home and I'll be with you".

Minutes later we were sprinting down Cambridge Road toward the beach. Sure enough, dotted along the tide-line were dark mounds of dead cattle surrounded by curious onlookers. I don't know why, but I expected to see the eyes of the dead beasts closed as though sleeping peacefully, so it came as a shock to find they were wide open and staring. Very soon we were joined by people pushing an assortment of carts, prams and wheelbarrows. Even a van or two trundled through breaks in the sand-hills! I was mystified as to why they had brought these means of transportation with them but in a relatively short time, it became abundantly clear. People began to carve up the animals and remove the choicest cuts of meat and it didn't take long to reduce them to unrecognisable heaps of bones.

One man, who had been particularly industrious, called on our help to load his van, for which we each received a three-penny 'joey' and a large piece of beef. It was a cold winter evening and gradually, as peoples enthusiasm began to wane and with the temperature dropping rapidly, they started to drift away. Light was fading fast and it soon became difficult to see, so taking a bearing on the tower of Christ Church, we started to make our way home. In the semi-darkness light glinted from axes and knives, as a few people continued to cut meat from the dead animals.

The authorities took an extremely dim view of the whole affair and instructed the police to arrest anyone removing meat from the shore. Although later, one or two people were arrested and charged, they didn't act quickly enough and on that first night tons of prime steak and brisket had been removed. The piece I had been given was, according to the man who gave it to me, 'the gear' and that 'yer mam will be made up with tha'! Unfortunately, my mam wasn't made up with it and said she wouldn't touch it with a docker's hook! Mick, on the other hand thoroughly enjoyed it and for the next few days was spoilt rotten!

Ultimately, a contractor was hired to remove the dead beasts from the sands and this continued over a period of days. However, the transit area where he stored them, prior to their disposal, became congested and so a few were left high and dry on the beach. It turned out to be a blessing in disguise for us, because when the animals became bloated, with their legs stick-ing grotesquely in the air, it provided us with a wonderful tram-poline and guaranteed us hours of fun! Its popularity spread rapidly and soon kids from all over Seaforth and Waterloo were competing against each other. The system was simple. You built up your running speed, hurtled up the sandy ramp, then, with a mighty bounce on the belly, you sailed through the air, hoping you could improve on your previous effort. Outstanding individual achievements were marked with a stick and, because the competitors were of such high standard there was a cluster of sticks all within a few inches of each other.

Eddie Bourne was extremely good at it and would take some beating. He was also extremely unlucky. Considering how popular the game was, it came as no surprise that in a relatively short time the fur on the hide wore away. Indeed, it became so transparent, you could see the animals inners! After school the following day, I was keen to get back down to the beach, but first I had to fetch a gas mantle from the chandler's for my mam. They were as fragile as cobwebs and had to be carried as though handling nitro-glycerin. I have, in the past, arrived home with a box that contained little more than a heap of white powder in the middle of a chalky collar! Consequentially, by the time I caught up with everyone, there was a long queue to bounce on the cow. Eddie was just ahead of me and he turned and waved as I approached.

"All right, Charlie" he said, rubbing his hands together excitedly. "I'm goin' to do my best t'night t' beat all 'ands". It was obvious that Eddie didn't consider me a threat to his chances of becoming overall champion and was casting sidelong glances at the opposition.

"Well," I ventured, "I can't see anyone here tonight that you need to worry about, Eddie."

"I dunno," he whispered from the corner of his mouth, "them two over there were quite good last night", and he nodded in the direction of two biggish lads with bulging leg muscles. I must admit, looking at Eddy's rather lithe form and mentally comparing it to both the lads he had pointed out, I didn't know either! But his record was there for all to see among the leading group of sticks.

"Well, you'll soon find out" I said, "its your turn next".

Eddie's wind-up was really something to see. His left leg went back as his head lowered close to his feet. He repeated it twice, then moved back and forth like a rocking horse, all the time emitting growling noises. He completed his preparations by shaking his head vigorously and puffing out his cheeks. Then, suddenly, he was off! It was a sight to see alright, and not one to forget. Sand flurries flew high in the air as he hit the ramp then his knees were up to his chest, ready for the final spring that would send him arcing through the air. Only he didn't arc! Instead, there was a squelching sound and Eddie disappeared up to his knees inside the cow!

What happened next isn't very clear. An awful stench invaded our nostrils and something prickled the back of our eyes causing them to water. Such was its potency, an old gentleman, who was strolling on the beach at the time, and a veteran of the first world war, demanded to know who was messing about with mustard gas! All that we could think of was to put as much space between ourselves and the abomination that had erupted from inside the cow, and before you could say 'what the hell is that' we had taken to our heels. In fact, I remember thinking that if I could have sprinted as well as that earlier, my stick might have been moved up among the leaders.

Comradeship is a wonderful thing and I believed I had it in abundance. Come what may, I thought, I would never desert a mate. Now I knew I lacked the moral fibre necessary to embrace undying friendship because nothing, but nothing, could have induced me to go back and assist Eddie to climb out of that cow! I knew now that I would yield under torture. In fact, the moment they wheeled in the trolley displaying the instruments required for extracting information, I would be singing like Al Jolson!

I last saw Eddie standing upright inside the cow with a look of bewildered disgust on his face and his arms outstretched as though pleading for help. As I put more distance between myself and Eddie, he reminded me of a naval officer standing in the Conning Tower of a submarine about to issue the order to 'dive, dive, dive'! The beach gradually became deserted, an alien world containing only Eddie and a variety of seagulls that dipped and wheeled as news of a new food supply spread among them.

Over the years, some strange things have drifted in on the tide. Occasionally, the odd channel buoy would break from its moorings and became a fantasy play-ground of rival pirate crews and fights over buried treasure, and sometimes even the odd porpoise would drift in! I think the strangest thing I ever saw washed up was a horse and cart! The horse was dead in the shafts complete with reins. Although there was nothing in the cart, it was thought it must have been used for cockling. As no-one in the immediate coastal region had reported one missing, the only other explanation put forward was that it had drifted over from Wales. I never knew the outcome of that strange and macabre wreckage and, sadly, it was removed before we could renew our 'tramp' competitions!

I also remember when thousands of oranges littered the shore, both loose and in wooden boxes, and I carted hundreds home. Unfortunately, the salt water had tainted most of them, but nevertheless, the vast majority were edible and at least half of what I salvaged were eventually eaten. I wonder if Eddie got any oranges? Come to think of it, I didn't see a lot of him after that. Someone told me he had taken a job on a farm and was doing great, which didn't surprise me. Well, as he'd demon-strated, he knew all about cows, inside and out!

Chapter 18

The snow beneath my feet was soft, crunchy and dazzling white. As I walked, little mounds formed on the ends of my goloshes, which were already very wet. It became necessary to walk with a slow, deliberate tread, avoiding slush where I could. Even in the few minutes I'd been out, my toes were beginning to tingle and my exposed thighs had a bluish tinge to them. The temptation to make snowballs was too great and I let fly at every lamp-post and tree branch I came across, trying to dislodge the snow clinging to them. After a while my hands became numb and I thrust them deep inside my trouser pockets to warm them. It was cold and I was thankful that my mam had pinned a scarf across my chest, 'because you're a bit chesty' she said.

As I turned into Cambridge Road a bus passed, spraying slushy snow across the pavement and spoiling the pristine surface. After picking up the few shivering passengers who were waiting at the bus stop, the conductor pressed the bell and the bus lurched forward, its ancient engine wheezing as it strained to pick up speed. It swayed alarmingly as it rounded the corner by the railway bridge and only missed the advertising hoardings by inches. I continued on down Dewlands Road, where the erection of the new 'pre-fabs' was taking place, and followed the barracks railings to Claremont Road. A clinking of glass caused me look across the road in time to see Mrs Roberts taking the milk from the step. She waved in recognition and shouted.

"The lads have already left. You'll catch them if you hurry" and with a final wave closed the door quickly to keep out the cold. The road to school was long and winding and buzzed with activity. People shouted greetings to each other and continued on their way, anxious to reach their destination. Others stood talking in groups discussing the rationing situation and the continuing problem of what to get for the tea. The bell above the door of 'Aggie's General Shop' in Ewart Road tinkled merrily and Mrs Hepple emerged, carefully carrying a jug of milk. Once, when I was very young, I went in and asked for some broken biscuits and innocently handed over a bag of shrapnel as payment. Without saying a word Aggie took the bag, studied it for a moment, then passed me a couple of very broken Marie biscuits!

I could hear shouting coming from inside the barracks. The wind carried most of what was being said away but someone was 'a 'orrible . . .' something or other. Judging from the tone of the voice, I was happy not to be on the receiving end! In summer I usually took my time going home and played 'ollies' in the gutter all the way. I was never aware of distance or time, which often resulted in a mild ticking off from my mam. In winter, though, it was different. The journey seemed to take twice as long and, even though it was cold, I made slow progress. Jingling the two pennies in my pocket, I would quicken my step in the direction of Dean's Cake Shop.

One day at school, we had been promised a special treat. We had all been told to bring a large container in order to receive some cocoa powder, sent to us from America. The largest container I could find was an old National Dried Food tin and although a bit rusty inside it would hold quite a bit. The sun had climbed a little higher and the snow began to melt and run in small rivulets into the gutter, where it flowed unseen under it's icy covering. At night the melting snow would freeze again, adding to the ever thickening icy surface.

Turning into School Lane by Arthur Watts Scrap Yard, I looked at the bombed site next to the GPO sorting depot. It looked picturesque in its fresh, white covering. Over by the houses near the railway the single track of an animal showed plainly, zig-zagging across the field. From the backyard wall of a nearby house, a cat watched me closely as I approached, wary and ready to turn tail and run. I think I preferred the field as it was then, in it's new winter outfit. It hid the ugliness of the rubble and scuffed areas beneath, where we played 'holey', a game of marbles. However, unless there was a rapid thaw, there would be no holey today! Instead, the main past-times during lunch hour would be snowball fights and ice sliding.

Johnny Mulvey was my best friend at school and like Kato in "The Pink Panther" films, he used to lie in wait and surprise attack me when I arrived. Once, I cautiously entered the school play-ground keeping a wary eye open and, clutching my ammo', made my way toward the toilets. My guess had been right because as I approached them, the doors burst open and Johnny charged out pelting me with snow. I was ready for him this time, though, and soon turned the tables. He retreated to the waste ground where we were soon involved in a pitched battle! In the end we were rolling around on the ground, trying to push snow inside each others shirt! It was only when we were laughing and brushing ourselves down that we suddenly realised we were alone and that everyone else had gone into school. We hadn't heard the bell in the heat of 'battle' and were late!

The headmaster, Mr Williams, who we called 'Wiggs' was waiting at the entrance as we raced through the gates. He pointed with his cane to a corner in the corridor where a few other pale faced lads were awaiting their fate.

"Wait over there," he said, indicating the group huddled in the corner, "and quietly!" he added, raising his voice. At five past nine he locked the main door then turned and faced us.

"Ah, Draper, I might have known you would be late. This must be the third time this week! And what is your excuse this time, eh?" he demanded.

"I didn't hear the bell, sir," I said "we were playing and . . ."

"Don't lie to me, boy," he shouted, "you can hear the bell for miles. The rest of the school heard it, but not you. Do you suffer from deafness?" he asked, but without waiting for a reply, added impatiently "hold out your hand".

I timorously extended my hand from my side, but he was having none of that. Pulling my arm to its full extent, he brought the cane down hard on my finger tips, an action he repeated four times. Unfortunately, because I 'fudged', the last one whacked me across the thumb, and I knew from bitter experience it would be the most painful when the numbness wore off!

"Now get to your class and don't let me see you here again," he said, "or next time it will be six!"

Johnny was next and I could hear the whacks of the cane as I stood around the corner waiting for him. I tucked my hands under my arm-pits, trying to warm them and doing my best to keep the tears from my eyes in case the other lads thought I was crying. I was soon joined by Johney who, with his hands tucked between his thighs, was puffing his cheeks out and like me, was trying not to cry! Half an hour later I had received another two whacks for not knowing the answer to a question from the catechism book, which happened regularly and used to frustrate me to distraction! Why should I be punished for not knowing the answer to a question? Helped, yes, but not punished.

At play-time, while everyone else was busy dodging snowball's, Johney and I sneaked out and made our way to the back of Allerton's Bakery in School Lane. Sometimes, if you were lucky, the bakers might leave the rear door of the bake-house open, allowing the bread and cakes to cool. Today, we were lucky! Laid out on a long table were rows and rows of freshly baked loaves and set to one side were trays of cakes and buns. We looked at each other and, after making sure the coast was clear, dashed in and grabbed a couple each! I had no idea what cakes I had stuffed up my jumper, but we raced back to school and headed straight for the toilets to scoff them! It turned out I had an eccles cake and a currant bun. Johnny had taken two custards which, considering how we had to 'leg it', were still in remarkable condition! I swapped him an eccles cake for a custard and we spent the rest of play-time stuffing ourselves and ignoring the pleas of lads outside wanting to come in for a 'wee'!

The remainder of the day passed, as most days did, with me staring uncomprehendingly at a maths problem on the blackboard. I was quite hopeless at 'sums' and as one of the slower ones I was left to do my best. I was thankful when, at ten minutes to four, we were told to line up with our tins and approach the desk one at a time. On a table near-by was a large carton emblazoned with the words,

"COLACT, THE WORLDS FINEST CHOCOLATE DRINK".

On the flap, next to a large american flag, two hands were clasped in friendship, above which it stated,

"A PRESENT FROM AMERICA"

Our teacher, Mrs Mallinson, scooped the chocolate powder into my tin and pulled a face when she noted its rusty interior! From there we moved to the next desk where we were handed a rosy, red apple. I had never seen an apple that was completely red before and it fascinated me. I'd been 'sappin' all over the district and never come across one so red! I polished it to a high gloss and put it in my pocket to keep it safe.

On my way home temptation got the better of me and I sat on the steps of the Sandown pub gorging myself on Colact, dipping a wet finger in and pulling it out covered in a thick layer of cocoa. I'm not sure how long I sat there sucking at my finger but my tin was considerably lighter than when I started out. I don't know if it was the world's finest chocolate drink or not, but it tasted pretty good to me! Its a good job it wasn't summer or I might well have eaten the lot, but my feet were freezing so I got up and continued on my way. I arrived home feeling very important as I handed it to my mam, and for a while we all enjoyed a hot cocoa night cap. The apple? Guess!

Chapter 19

I often marvel at a pigeon's homing instinct. As a lad I remember trapping half a dozen thinking I would help with the family budget by 'growing' my own eggs! They turned out to be such prodigious egg-layers that I couldn't cope and as a consequence, baby pigeons started hatching all over the place! Very soon my flock became unmanageable, making it difficult to look after them properly, and it became obvious steps had to be taken in order to resolve the situation. My dad, although he tolerated animals, was no Francis Of Assisi, and slung the lot out on their ear! It was many months before my brood accepted the fact that food wasn't forthcoming as readily as it used to, and with nowhere to snuggle up at night, decided to vacate the area. I breathed a sigh of relief when the last pigeon cocked a snook at me and left, because the corporation yard opposite was beginning to resemble Trafalgar Square!

It came as a complete surprise when a couple of years later, a single pigeon appeared out of the blue and took up residence on one of our back bedroom window ledges. Why it chose that particular window ledge out of the selection available in the locality, is beyond me. I mean, ours were nothing to write home about. Just plain stone ledges. Now, three doors down at Mrs Chambers, they were what you would call window ledges. In the 'AA Pigeon Fanciers Hand-Book' her ledges would warrant three, possibly four stars! They were stout, substantial ledges and, in fact, two of them were situated near the outlet of a coal burning stove. Infinitely superior to what I could offer a wing-weary traveller! It isn't as though I encouraged it. There were no notices stating,

"TIRED PIGEON'S WELCOME. BED AND CORN, DROP IN!"
However, this particular pigeon had decided this was the place for him. Undeterred by my arm flapping antics it settled down,

waggled its tail a few times, and began to doze off! When my dad saw it he thought I was up to my old tricks again and gave me a dressing down in the garden. I assured him I wasn't, but he still tore a strip off me, ending with the words ". . . if you don't get rid of that" pointing to the bird, "I will." It was a threat which left me in no doubt as to the outcome and I wished I could have conveyed it to the bird sitting contentedly on the ledge. I am certain he would have packed his bags and left before you could say `pigeon pie'!

As pigeons do not like flying at night, they very sensibly pass away the dark hours by sleeping. I simply waited until dark, opened the window, grabbed Dennis as I christened him, and placed his unresisting form in a box until morning. The following day I was up and out of the house before anyone else had stirred. Tying the box containing a very muted pigeon to my bike, I pedalled like mad to the only place I could think of where he would feel at home, the docks. There were hundreds of pigeons near an old grain elevator, just past the Gladstone Dock gate and when I released him he coo'd and clucked as he walked among them. He puffed out his chest as if saying, 'you'll never guess what happened to me!' Dennis seemed content prancing around eating his fill of spilled grain, and I arrived home feeling rather smug in the certain knowledge that I could tell my dad the situation had been resolved.

The grin on my face froze solid when a single 'coo' made me look up to the window ledge and I saw him sitting there. He looked down at me with his head cocked to one side as if to say 'what kept you?' I couldn't believe it and even Mick my dog, had a bemused look on his face! This needed thinking about and I sat on the step to try and formulate a plan.

I was mystified. Here was a pigeon, grabbed off a ledge in the middle of the night, put in a box, and taken to a place it had no doubt never seen before, and it beat me home! I resolved to put an end to this nonsense once and for all. Especially before my dad got wind of it! So Dennis, who really had become a menace, had to go and this time for keeps!

That evening I followed the same procedure as the night previous and next morning I was up and out and pedalling like a lunatic. Only this time I went in a different direction. This time, I headed to Crosby. I argued that if pigeons are guided by the sun, which I believe they are, and if he keeps it on his left shoulder, or wing, then in a few hours from now he would be scouring the streets of Southport looking for our house. Cunning eh? That's what makes us superior to the rest of the animal kingdom, we have cunning in abundance!

I liberated him in Coronation Park near the bowling greens. People were throwing bread and handfuls of seed and he fluttered among them, eating his fill and strutting around. There were plenty of other pigeons he could natter to so while his attention was diverted, I hopped on my bike and sloped off. When I arrived home I looked tentatively at the ledge but, thankfully, it was vacant.

Later that evening as I was stacking some timber ready for sawing, I heard a slapping of wings and Dennis, looking extremely pleased with himself, hovered for a moment before gently touching down on the ledge!

I couldn't believe my eyes and in my frustration threw down a piece of wood I'd been holding. I watched helplessly as it bounced and executed a perfect triple salco through the back kitchen window. Unfortunately, the window was closed at the time! The resulting crash of glass brought everyone running outside thinking I had gone completely mad. My dad grabbed me by the scruff of the neck and demanded to know what I was playing at. I tried to explain but all that came out was gibberish, so I was sent to my room 'until I get around to sorting you out'!

I went to the room where Dennis, who really was a menace, had taken up residence and opened the window with no other purpose in mind than to shove him off, but as I did so he hopped inside and perched on the mantelpiece. I went over and picked him up intent on exacting some sort of revenge for getting me into so much trouble. He offered no resistance at all and any malice I had felt toward him earlier, vanished in that one instant. I held him in the crook of my arm, gently stroking his feathers. He didn't resist in any way and it gave me an opportunity to really look at him. I was surprised to see just how colourful he was. He wasn't a flashy looking pigeon like some I'd seen. In fact, he was pretty drab looking really, but the feathers around his neck appeared to include all the colours of the rainbow, and gradually I began to warm to Dennis.

It was much later when my mam shouted me down for my tea and as I was eating I kept glancing to my dad wondering, and hoping, if he had forgotten about 'sorting me out'. He gave no indication either way and carried on reading his Echo but when I looked at my mam she winked and smiled. At last he put the paper down and looked over at me.

"Your Mam seems to think we should let you keep that bird." I started to speak but he held up his hand, "I'm not sure that she's right, but I'm willing to see how you go on. You will have to build a hutch or something for it and take care of it and it'll be your responsibility, and yours only. Oh, there's one other thing," and he leaned forward to emphasise his point, "there will only ever be the one. Is that understood? I don't want to go out there one day and see that some of his mates have decided to keep him company. Not even an egg! Understand? Not an egg!" He went back to reading his paper and I looked at my mam. She just winked again and nodded.

While my dad had been telling me about the do's and don't's, in my minds eye I already had a hutch outlined! Jimmy and Ronnie would help and we'd soon knock one up. In the end we didn't have to. Arty had an old rabbit hutch which he said I could have, on the condition that he could hold `the little guy' now and then. We set to work on it and by extending the top, to give it extra height and lengthening the legs, it turned out to be just the job!

Dennis was with me for years. Even Mick accepted him,

although with a certain amount of reluctance, and very often Dennis would sit on his back for a free ride! At night I used to open the window and he would fly up and perch on my headboard and stay there till morning, then come first light he'd fly back to his hutch. It was as though he knew he'd get me in trouble if he was found there! I think he was a frustrated parrot, because he liked to perch on my shoulder as I walked around the garden. Unlike a dog, you couldn't take him for walks or wrestle with him, but he was good company in many ways. If I was playing football in the street he would sit on the roof watching and occasionally coo his approval if I scored a goal!

One night he failed to fly into my room and when I went down to investigate, I found him dead. The next morning, Ronnie, Jimmy and I buried him in the garden near some old incendiary bombs. It was a simple ceremony. Wearing our specially made paper hats we fired three rounds into the air from our brush-poles, then marched silently away. Dennis was an intruder who found a home with me and has remained with me ever since.

Chapter 20

In the summer of 1947, I went 'abroad' to New Brighton. Well, that's how it seemed to me at the time. It was across the sea on a boat. The fact that the boat was a ferry and only travelled about two miles is immaterial. I'd never been there before and as far as I was concerned, it was abroad!

My dad had promised us a day out to New Brighton when he was able and when he could afford it, and now we were going! The day of our departure dawned warm and sunny and preparations for an early start were well under way by the time I finally emerged from the cupboard under the stairs. I'd been searching for my bucket and spade! It had been a case of location by touch in the dark recess but when viewed in the cold light of day, I found it very much the worse for wear. It had somehow managed to survive the bombing during the war but hadn't fared too well under a peace-time barrage of working boots and mop buckets. However, once I had subjected it to a severe pounding with a hammer, it became an acceptable oval shape. The seam was split in a couple of places, but viewed from a certain angle I didn't expect my sand pies would attract too many unfavourable comments. Everything we had packed for the trip, sandwiches, lemonade, and various other items was double checked. Then my mam nodded.

"I think we've got everything" she said, tucking a wet flannel into the corner of bag, "so let's be off." My sister Ann and I were soon out of the house and waiting impatiently outside! Dad locked the door and after a re-assuring pat of his pocket to make sure he had his 'Woodies', we were off.

The bus ride to Seaforth Sands Station was a short one and as soon as we stepped down from the bus my sister and I bounded up the stairs to the elevated platform of the Overhead Railway. Because Seaforth Sands was the terminus, it was always crowded with people. Some were taking the opportunity to enjoy a panoramic view of the docks, but most were setting off on the first leg of a journey to New Brighton. When the train pulled in there was the inevitable mad rush to get a 'speck' by the window which would overlook the docks as we travelled along.

The carriages and slatted seats were made of wood and smelled of pipe tobacco and polish, which over the years had stained the white painted, domed ceiling, yellow. The journey was wonderful and as the train rattled along, following the line of docks, it was almost possible to see into the ship's funnels. My dad, being a docker and an ex-seaman, pointed out the different type of ships and what kind of cargo they would carry. He also explained the markings painted on the funnels, which was usually the company logo or house flag.

From my elevated position I was able to observe what was happening at ground level and I have never forgotten it! In one dock, a grain elevator could be seen shrouded in a fine yellow dust as it sucked wheat, like a huge vacuum cleaner, from deep inside the hold of a ship. In another dock, two tugs were busy coaxing a large liner gently onto her berth. Men and vehicles bustled everywhere. Horse drawn carts were far more common in those days and teams of sweating horses could be seen pulling loads up and down cobbled avenues between warehouses. Ships derricks swung cases and bales from their holds and landed them on mobile electric bogies, which then ran the cargo into the dock-side warehouse where it was sorted and stacked.

All too soon the train rattled into the Pier Head Station and doors banged open as excited holiday makers poured onto the platform. Once our tickets had been punched, we ran down the stairs and followed the happy, laughing crowds to the floating landing stage. At that time it was the biggest in the world and its size was reflected in the number of vessels that could berth there! Not only could it accommodate the Mersey ferries and the Isle Of Man and North Wales steamers, but also some of the worlds largest passenger liners! A rail link ran into the Princes Dock where passengers could embark directly onto the ship with the minimum of fuss.

The landing stage was constructed to rise and fall as the tide determined while still allowing ships to tie up when required. The tide was out when we arrived and the covered ramps leading down to the landing stage were very steep, causing people to lean back in order to prevent themselves from breaking into a run! Once on the stage I looked back. There was an expanse of brown oozing mud between where we stood and the Pier Head wall. Hanging in a gentle curve, partly immersed, were massive chains, their links filled with black mud. These kept the pontoons in check and were made fast by large cleats cut into the quayside. The landing stage still exists today, but much reduced in size.

"Look!" shouted my sister excitedly, "here comes our ship!" My dad tried to explain that it wasn't a ship, but a ferry boat that would take us to New Brighton.

"But it's a ship!" we both protested. "Its the same as all those over there," and we pointed to the ships in the river waiting at anchor. My dad tried to explain the difference between a ship and a boat, but in the end gave it up as a bad job.

"You're right," he said in resignation, "here comes our ship!"

It seemed to me the ferry approached the landing stage at a fair old lick and I wondered if it would stop in time. At the last second, though, it seemed to put on the brakes and she drifted against the stage with a gentle bump. We stood waiting with our feet a few inches away from a brass metal strip screwed to the planking. This was the point where the ramp would come to rest when it was lowered. And lower it certainly did! I expected a controlled descent but it came down with a bang and bounced around a bit before finally coming to rest.

There were two ramps, one at the stern and one a little forward of mid-ships. We were at the stern and when most of the passengers were off, we ran on board. It was a time of great excitement and we ran up the stairs to the top deck so that once we cast off we could throw bread to the seagulls. Finding a space on the rail we looked down at the water, our eyes wide with fascination as my dad pointed out various landmarks. Almost immediately there was a clanging of bells, which was repeated somewhere deep inside the ship and men lifted the ramps. Suddenly, the water below us erupted! The river boiled frothy white but beyond the propellers' furious thumping, it smoothed to a chocolate brown. Happening as quickly as it did took me by surprise and recognising the power beneath my feet, it felt a little scary. At the same time the ropes which held us to the quayside were pulled in and our ship became independent of the land. We were at sea!

Dodging in and out of vessels anchored in the river we watched as New Brighton loomed nearer. The fairground was clearly visible and we could hear screams coming from people riding the Big Dipper. As soon as the ramp hit the quayside, Ann and I were racing up the covered bridge that led to the promenade. To our left a band was playing and people danced in the warm, open air. We were just in time to see the one-legged diver climb to a platform high above a tank filled with water. I watched mesmerised as the crowd below cheered him on and he launched himself into space. Water cascaded over the crowd when he dived into the tank and a moment later he climbed out to a thunderous applause! I had never seen anything like it and my mouth was still open when we arrived at the fair!

We didn't spend a lot of time there because my dad didn't have much money. We had a go on some of the rides and we were content with that. Besides, there was plenty to see that cost nothing. The motor cycle riders in the 'Wall Of Death' for a start! It was a thrilling exhibition of skill and daring, because occasionally the riders came so close to the top of the 'wall' I felt sure one of them was going to fly out! Eventually, my mam and dad decided it was time to go to the beach and relax and where I could make lots of oval-shaped sand-pies!

At Blackpool and Southport, they could brag of 'miles of golden sands', but New Brighton's beaches were small sandy patches between the rocks! The two most popular stretches of sand were either side of the pier and were always crowded. There was barely space enough to spread a towel, let alone play games. However, people jostled an inch here and there and very soon a space became available. Where New Brighton had an advantage over both Blackpool and Southport was the distance to the sea. There, if you went looking for the sea when the tide was out, you had to take sandwiches and a flask of tea with you! Here, it was a short haul with my leaking bucket carrying water to fill the moat around my castle. I had just made another unsuccessful attempt to make a sand-pie when my dad shouted to me.

"Charlie! Come on, lets me and you go for a walk."

We walked along the beach toward the open air swimming pool and I could see people diving off the high board. It looked very dangerous to me and I marvelled at the skill they showed. We watched for a while, listening to the cheers of the crowds inside as each diver completed a difficult sequence. We then saw a strange tank-like vehicle move along the sand, enter the water and float like a boat! I'd never seen anything like it. My dad saw the expression on my face and explained that it was used for landing troops and supplies on the beaches during the war and that it was as much at home in water as on land. It was an ex-American DUKW and painted in military green with a big white star on each side. Because of its name it was known as a 'duck'!

My dad rendered me speechless by asking me if I'd like a go. Would I like a go! I couldn't think of anything I'd like more! We walked over to where a man wearing a seaman's cap and a leather satchel over his shoulder was shouting.

"Last chance today to have a trip in a genuine veteran of

Normandy. Come on, folks, treat the kids to a great ride!" We walked to where a group of people stood waiting.

"Just you and the lad, sir?" the man asked my dad. "That'll be 'one an' a 'tanner'"

The 'duck' suddenly surged onto the beach with water streaming down its sides. Its wheels gripped the sand and before I knew it, it was pulling alongside and I was climbing on board! I was able to sit up front behind the driver and when we were full, he put it in gear and we rolled down the beach toward the river! It was a terrific sensation when we entered the water and pulled away from the beach. I wished with all my heart that we could keep going all the way across and run onto Seaforth Sands! I could imagine the faces of the people on the beach as I drove past them! All too soon it was over and I was climbing down the ladder onto the sand.

When we got back to my mam I couldn't shut up about it and told her in detail where we went, how we went and described what it felt like. I suppose I must have gone on a bit.

"That sounds smashing," she said, "maybe I'll come next time. Tell you what, I'm awful thirsty! See that van by the pier? You take Ann and get us all a nice pot of tea, eh?" The 'duck' ride was certainly one of the highlights of the day and I couldn't wait to get back to Jimmy and Ronnie to tell them. They'd never had a go on one, and in fact hadn't even seen one! A few weeks ago Jimmy had bragged about his trip through the tunnel when he went to Wales. Well, if this doesn't top that, I don't know what will! At the very least I should squeeze a few 'ollies' out of them!

Another highlight, and not one of my making, was almost getting myself into a fight. It also very nearly got me into a lot of trouble! I was returning with yet another bucket of water for my moat, when a lad about my age walked over and jumped all over my castle! Well, I wasn't having that. I shouted at him and when he saw me coming, he legged it. I was quickly in hot pursuit! With the beach being so crowded it wasn't easy to run and I trampled over more than one prone figure in my eagerness to get to grips with the fleeing figure ahead of me. I would have done too, but disaster struck! A woman carrying ice creams in one hand and what turned out to be a plate of sandwiches in the other, stepped in front of me and I crashed into her, head on. I hadn't realised the carnage I had left strewn in my wake. Babies were crying, little girls were reassuring their dolls that all was well, and mams and dads were brushing sand from their hair and eyes, while giving me 'daggers'! I was hauled to my feet by my dad who would have been reaching for his belt if he'd been wearing one! Either way I was going to cop it and waited for the first stinging slap until a lady came over and told him what had happened.

"So really," she concluded, "although he caused chaos running through the crowd like he did, he was provoked. Don't be too hard on him, will you?" Her words seemed to have a calming effect on my dad because he looked down at me.

"You can thank this lady," he said, "that you're not getting a hiding, my lad. I'll give you the benefit of the doubt this time, now go away, stay in sight and stay out of trouble." I could have kissed her!

I spent the rest of the afternoon looking for crabs in little pools and kept well out of the way of my dad in case he changed his mind and gave me a clip around the ear, anyway! I wandered around collecting shellfish and crabs until my bucket was over-flowing. I wanted to take them home but as my bucket leaked like a sieve this wasn't possible. There were no plastic bags in those days to line it with and so I returned them to their natural environment. When I saw my mam shaking her towel and packing the bags, I knew that my day out was coming to an end.

It was a wonderful day. I'd had a train ride along the docks, a trip on a 'ship', an adventure on a 'duck' and a few hours on the beach. All in one day! I'd never been further than a bus ride to Formby or Freshfield before and I knew I'd never forget it. And, of course, I haven't.

Chapter 21

The sound echoed around the lobby, rumbled down the street and bounced noisily between the gables of near-by houses. Dogs howled, cats fled and music lovers everywhere raised petitions in protest. My dad was playing the piano!

He couldn't play for nuts, but to the inebriated revellers whirling and dancing in our front parlour he was a melodic cocktail of Liberace, Mrs Mills and Russ Conway!

Once, he received compensation for a bad dock injury and declared his intention to buy a piano. My sister Mary also expressed a desire to learn and so the matter was settled. Soon a shiny, upright piano, was delivered by Rushworth and Dreaper and placed in the front parlour. Before the delivery men had climbed back into their van, a doily appeared as if by magic and a vase of tulips, in dire need of liquid refreshment, was placed on top. There was a mad rush for the piano stool because, of course, we all wanted 'to have a go'!

My dad spent an hour or so most evenings 'tickling the ivories', and my mam spent most of the day polishing them! According to his inner ear, each note was in its correct place, but to the rest of the family, taking refuge in various parts of the house, it sounded awful. It was so bad my sister Amy, returning home after a night out, asked why dad was smashing up the new piano!

The war had been over for a couple of years and people had begun to look ahead to a brighter future. Gradually, the war receded into the back of their minds. Our house at the time was always a lively place and was the scene for many a 'do'. The front door was open and stayed open for anyone who happened to be passing to come in and join in the fun. And they did!

Neither my mam or dad drank much, but at weekends they would pass an hour away in the Doric Pub on Rawson Road and meet with their friends. Usually, they would invite people back to the house for, as my mam put it, 'a sing-song and a get-together'. Meanwhile, at home, my sisters prepared sandwiches and kept the kettle boiling in constant readiness. After they left the Doric and turned into our road, their imminent arrival was broadcast from the other end of the street by rousing renditions of the most popular tunes of the day. Mick, who recognised a good tune when he heard one, made straight for his kennel!

As the party got into full swing I used to edge my way inside the parlour and watch as various people performed their party piece. My two elder brothers, Stanley and David, would do their 'Sand Dance' routine and my sisters, who had good voices, sang 'Trees' and 'When I'm Calling You'. There was also Mr Pendle, who loved to yodel, play the spoons and pluck at the banjo. All at the same time! I used to like listening to Ernie, the Royal Navy's Donald Peers. He looked splendid in his uniform singing 'By A Babbling Brook'. Once, an American who was passing, heard the music and came in. He was smashing and sang Country and Western songs. That was the first time I heard Hank Williams' songs and his kind of music. On another occasion, three sisters from down the road came in and impersonated the 'Andrew Sisters' with a sterling rendition of 'Mister-What-You-Call-It'! Mr Sinclair, who later became Father Sinclair, was a big hit whistling bird impressions to, appropriately enough, 'In a Monastery Garden'!

A big favourite of mine was Mr Gould who was not gifted as a performer but sat in the corner applauding every turn and would endorse his appreciation by lowering large quantities of drink. His scale of 'one to ten' was gauged by how long his mouth pulled at the bottle. He must have thought Lydia, the soprano who sang `One Fine Day' from Puccini's 'Madame Butterfly' was wonderful, because his mouth remained fastened to a bottle of Scotch like a limpet! I watched fascinated as he became more and more incapable. If he noticed me watching him he would wink, put his thumb up and make whistling and clicking noises. However, it was when he tried to go home he provided the best entertainment!

In the years that followed I came across drunks in many different parts of the world. They all had their own style, their own way of reaching their eventual destination. Legs, quivering and stalling like a car engine, would suddenly splutter into life and straighten momentarily, allowing them to make slow, but definite progress. Even those who veered from side to side like the ball in a pin-ball machine sometimes made you hold your breath, but they all had that wonderful capacity to survive!

A well known drunk in Waterloo was noted for his ability to dance like Fred Astaire, irrespective of how much he had to drink. He would perform a marvellous routine of high stepping and twirling. His finale, was to tap dance up and down the steps of Waterloo Station. He was outstanding. The problem started when he finished his act. His legs turned to jelly and he found it impossible to walk a straight line! The last time I saw 'Fred' he was trying to board a train and was fighting a losing battle with the automatic doors!

Once, I went to stay with a friend of mine who lived in Seaforth Road and from our vantage point in his bedroom we could watch the antics of drunks as they weaved their way along the road. After spending an hour in the Caradoc they would stagger to the Castle and have a few there, then back again to the Caradoc! For the rest of the night Seaforth Road was a hive of activity as people weaved their way erratically between pubs!

Our attention was drawn toward two particular drunks who, recognising each other, exchanged greetings.

"Now, 'arry!" shouted one.

"Alright, Tom?" Harry answered, "'ow's the missus?"

After a short while, and quite a few pints later, they passed again and waved cheerily to each other.

"'arry!"

"Tom!"

As the night wore on and the recognition of individuals

became more difficult, they mumbled something to the hazy figure in front of them and groped their way forward, ricocheting off shop windows and street signs! When they met just before 'last orders', a dim recollection, buried deep in the dark recesses of their minds, caused them to circle each other warily before continuing on their way. Eventually, the inevitable happened. As they passed for the last time on their way home, they collided! Words and threats were exchanged as they staggered around trying to disrobe! Having discarded their coats, they faced each other hiccoughing and belching. Flicking at their noses with their thumb, they threatened to thrash one another, but it wasn't to be. They both aimed a punch, missed, and slumped to the ground, out cold! A couple of men from the crowd, who expressed their disappointment at not seeing a good fight, dragged them to their feet and propped them against a wall to sober up! Some time later, 'Big Sam' the local beat bobby, came along and carted them off to Seaforth Police Station to sleep it off !

Seaforth Road at that time was being subjected to major sewerage works and down the centre was a deep, shuttered trench. It was during the days when the fencing of obstacles never really entered the heads of contractors, even when a simple sign stating 'Keep Off' was all that was required! This being the case, it is not surprising that many a drunk fell into the trench. It must have seemed like falling into the Grand Canyon! Undaunted, they would often quite happily curl up in one of the large pipes and go to sleep until they sobered up or were discovered by workmen the next morning! I often wonder what one man was thinking about when he emerged from the mouth of a pipe shouting, "I'm free, I'm free!" We had a cracking time watching it all unfold!

At our house there was a different scenario. One chap was leaving the party after trying to revive himself with cups of tea.

"Right then, I'm off." Shunning the attention of friends as they tried to steady him, he added, "its alright, I only live in

Chestnut Avenue. I'll trot home!" Stretching to his full height, he jogged away. After some twenty yards or so he began to jog backwards in a curious arm waving motion, then forward again. He continued this pattern of running for quite some time until, exhausted, he fell down and had to be carried home!

Mr Gould, on the other hand, was unique. The nerves that sent messages to his legs to support him had failed to deliver, a sure sign that there was a fault on the line! His legs turned into foam rubber and he became a sort of Zebadee character, rising and falling like a faulty marionette! After crashing through the hedge a couple of times, he would stare fixedly at me.

"I'm alight, boy," he used to say. "I'll be OK as soo' as get to the Fi' Lam'. I can gerra' bus there!" He used to wobble up the road in a slow, deliberate manner, delicately poised on his spring-like legs, pushing himself upright from the gate posts as he went. On one occasion I followed him to the Five Lamps to make sure he arrived alright and watched from a distance as he boarded the bus. It was an obvious challenge to him and I could hear him muttering and cursing as he grabbed the bar to pull himself up.

"Stan' back, stan' back! Keep it still a minute, pal! I've got it now!" and after a few abortive attempts to haul himself onto the platform, he finally managed to clatter onto the stairs. Winking and clicking and pointing to no-one in particular, he lurched inside and slumped onto the nearest seat! I watched as the bus gained momentum and noticed that his head had already slumped onto his chest and he was fast asleep! The bus swayed and lurched toward Seaforth and was soon enveloped in a sulphurous mist and all that could be seen was the ghostly yellow light from the windows and the winking of the traffic lights by Potter's Barn.

As it turned out I never saw Mr Gould after that. I don't know what happened to him, he just stopped coming. We still threw the odd party and they were still joyous occasions but something was missing; that little something that made my sides ache with laughter, the mental pictures that caused me to laugh when I was curled up in bed trying to sleep.

I remember once lying in bed listening to someone singing 'Red, Red Robin' as I fought against sleep. I was thinking of the next day because Jimmy, Ronnie and me had made plans to go bird-nesting and I desperately needed to find a moorhen's egg for my collection . . . or was it a robins? I'd sort it out in the morning!

Chapter 22

It is fair to say that every neighbourhood has its characters; some people stand out from the crowd and others are just regarded as being odd. It may be a strangeness in their behaviour, an unusual lifestyle or simply a mannerism. Either way, tongues will wag, fingers will point and that person is labelled forever. As a young boy I cast my label. It fluttered in the breeze then pirouetted once or twice before landing gently at the feet of 'Woodbine Effie'.

As I recall Effie seemed a lonely soul, a fact borne out by our next door neighbour, Mrs Turton, who referred to her as a 'poor old dear', Mrs Baxendale, whose voice always lowered to a confidential whisper said she 'was more to be pitied', and Mrs Poole, who muttered something about 'bombs' and 'the war' and tut-tutted into her cup of tea. No-one remembers seeing visitors call at her house, not even the usual callers like milkmen or coalmen. All of which added to the mysterious image Effie left in my mind.

Her house seemed to be in permanent darkness. No lights filtered through the grimy windows with their dirty, torn net curtains. The small path leading to the front door was carpeted with weeds, and flanking the doorway two overgrown rhododendrons swayed and embraced each other whenever the wind blew. To my young eyes Effie was an awesome sight, tall and lean with lank grey hair hanging down her back. She had a brown, wrinkled face with the inevitable Woodbine dangling from her puckered mouth. Effie seemed to possess only one coat which she wore summer and winter. It was long and black with a matted and tatty fur collar. Her thin bony legs moved with quick pitter patter steps and on her feet she wore a pair of mens boots over thick woolly socks rolled down to her ankles.

If I had to pass Effie in the street I would skirt around her and a pair of black eyes would flick once in my direction. Without breaking stride she would continue on her shuffling walk, while I ran as fast as my trembling knees allowed. To the boys in our gang Effie was a witch. She was different, so she became a target for us to taunt and make fun of. We were children and we were cruel. Sometimes we watched for her returning from the shops clutching her straw basket and fall in behind her chanting in sing song fashion, "Effie's a witch! Effie's a witch!".

She would turn and shake a scrawny fist as we took to our heels shrieking with laughter. Once, when there was enough of us in number to bolster our courage, we sneaked around to Effie's back garden, certain we would catch her at work casting spells and mixing awful smelling brews. It was on such a night, which we called Mischief Night, but is now Halloween, that we went to Effie's and worked our way through the undergrowth that was her garden. It was all bushes and hanging vines and something heaped in the corner which steamed and made noises and smelt awful. Some bright spark suggested that we take a look through the kitchen window. It was decided, unanimously, that it would be me. It wasn't that I was braver than anyone else. In fact, I would willingly have foregone the dubious pleasure, but I was the smallest and, it was argued, the lightest to hoist to the high window.

Peering over the sill into the dimly lit room I saw Effie sitting in a rocking chair opposite a glowing fire. A cat was curled sleepily on her lap and with her feet on a brass fender she pushed herself to and fro.   A spluttering gas mantle suspended from the ceiling cast sinister looking shadows around the room. I could hear faint sounds coming from an unseen radio and on a stove in the corner a kettle boiled, issuing little puffs of steam from its spout. The cat jumped from Effies lap, stretched in a contented manner and began lapping milk from a saucer next to a wooden coal scuttle.

"Tell us what you can see, Charlie!" pleaded one of my friends below.

"Hurry up" said another, " my shoulders are killing me!"

"Shush!" I said bending down, "she'll hear you". I turned back for another look and Effie's face was pressed to the window trying to see through the grime. I recoiled in horror and shouted as I fell through space. My friends had let go of me and bolted. I scrambled to my feet and raced through the gate as Effie's front door was opening.

"Wilful children!" I heard her shout, but I was off and running like a gazelle. The hairs on my neck stood out like pine needles as any second I felt sure a claw-like hand was about to clamp on my shoulders. My imagination ran riot, came along-side and overtook me. I was sure I could smell cigarette smoke in the night air and increased my running speed to Olympic standard.

I flew down Sandringham Road, skidded through the gateway of the corporation yard and hurled myself behind a heap of cobblestones. My heart was thumping in my chest and I got scared because Jimmy Telfer said that sometimes it thumped into your mouth and you had to spit it out and then you died. I was breathing hard but tried not to in case she heard me. I imagined her hunting me with a big stick, poking into dark corners. 'Come out, boy! I want you!' my mind whispered.

Much later, when my breathing became more controlled, I looked about me. It was quiet and still. My knees hurt where I'd scraped them as I landed on the gravel path. Spitting and blowing on them was good but tomorrow I'd find a dock leaf to rub them. That would take the sting away. It was a while before I moved from my hiding place and longer still before I reached home.

In the weeks to follow I occasionally saw Effie coming or going to the shops, her unmistakable walk causing the cigarette in her mouth to bob up and down. However, I kept a reason-able distance between us for fear she would recognise me.

One saturday morning as I ran to the Matinee Club at the Odeon Cinema on Crosby Road, I stumbled and the sixpence I had clutched in my hand went spinning away, rolling some distance, before tinkling down a grid. I was stunned. I looked into the grid where the water was still settling hoping it would somehow be floating on the surface. A straw-clutching thought! All the pulling and tugging at the grid cover was in vain. It was stuck fast. I sat on the kerb opposite the Five Lamps and the tears began to flow. Tears of self pity more than anything else, as I'd worked hard to get that sixpence, running errands and collecting lemonade bottles.

Now it was gone. I sat there crying and wiping my eyes with the back of my hand. There was a movement behind me and then a soft voice said

"What's up, son?". I just shook my head wiped my eyes and transferred the wetness to my shorts. A hand squeezed my shoulder gently. "Come on, tell me what happened". In between splutters and sniffles I related my tale of woe. After a moment or two, a shiny silver sixpence was pressed into my hand.

"Stop crying now and get along to your pictures". I spluttered a 'thank you' and looked up into Effie's face. She smiled. "Go on, you'll be late" she said, then turned and pitter-patted away. I watched as Effie's receding figure shimmered through the film of moisture in my eyes and felt a warm glow of affection for her and I think maybe at that point, I began to grow up.